The Mysterious  & Unknown

ESP

by Peggy J. Parks

ReferencePoint Press™

San Diego, CA

For more information, contact
ReferencePoint Press, Inc.
PO Box 27779
San Diego, CA 92198
www.ReferencePointPress.com

Picture credits:
AP/Wide World Photos, 22, 43, 47, 49, 57
Oscar Burriel/Science Photo Library, 8
Dreamstime, 11, 14
James Randi Educational Foundation, 83
Photos.com, 6
Science Photo Library, 17, 20, 29
Rob Stephney, 27
Jeremy Walker/Science Photo Library, 71
Steve Zmina, 24

Series design and book layout:
Amy Stirnkorb

LIBRARY OF CONGRESS CATALOGING-IN-PUBLICATION DATA

Parks, Peggy J., 1951-
  ESP / by Peggy J. Parks.
     p. cm. -- (Mysterious and unknown)
  Includes bibliographical references and index.
  ISBN-13: 978-1-60152-025-8 (hardback)
  ISBN-10: 1-60152-025-5 (hardback)
  1. Extrasensory perception--Juvenile literature. I. Title.
  BF1321.P38 2007
  133.8--dc22
                              2007009024

Contents

FOREWORD

"Strange is our situation here upon earth."
—*Albert Einstein*

Since the beginning of recorded history, people have been perplexed, fascinated, and even terrified by events that defy explanation. While science has demystified many of these events, such as volcanic eruptions and lunar eclipses, some continue to remain outside the scope of the provable. Do UFOs exist? Are people abducted by aliens? Can some people see into the future? These questions and many more continue to puzzle, intrigue, and confound despite the enormous advances of modern science and technology.

It is these questions, phenomena, and oddities that Reference-Point Press's *The Mysterious & Unknown* series is committed to exploring. Each volume examines historical and anecdotal evidence as well as the most recent theories surrounding the topic in debate. Fascinating primary source quotes from scientists, experts, and eyewitnesses, as well as in-depth sidebars further inform the text. Full-color illustrations and photos add to each book's visual appeal. Finally, source notes, a bibliography, and a thorough index provide further reference and research support. Whether for research or the curious reader, *The Mysterious & Unknown* series is certain to satisfy those fascinated by the unexplained.

INTRODUCTION

The Sixth Sense

On September 4, 2001, at 3:00 A.M., Becky Carter was jolted out of a deep sleep by a terrifying dream. All she could see in the dream was spinning blackness, but she heard a man's voice speaking to her. Over and over he repeated the same number, 2830, and then he kept saying a name that sounded like "Rooks" or "Horooks." As his voice grew louder and more urgent, Carter knew he was trying to tell her something, but she had no idea what. When she woke from the dream, the voice was still clear in her head, and she grabbed a pen and paper and scribbled down the number and name. Later that morning she said to her husband, a prosecuting attorney in North Carolina, "John, something's going to happen."[1]

During the following week, Carter could not stop thinking about the haunting voice and the name and number that made no sense. Then, on September 11, 2001, she suddenly understood. Hijacked by terrorists, United Airlines flight 175 slammed into the World Trade Center in New York City. As Carter watched the horrifying news on television, she heard the copilot's name—Michael Horrocks—and she was sure it was the name she had

Did You
Know?

ESP is most easily
defined as the
ability to perform
tasks outside the
normal human
senses by tapping
into the power of
the human mind.

The Twin Towers in New York City, before it was leveled by a terrorist attack in 2001. Becky Carter dreamed of the attack just days before it happened.

heard in her dream. There was no mention of the number 2,830, but she knew it had to mean something.

Just over eight months later, she found the missing piece of her puzzle. On May 15, 2002, a research paper that focused on the September 11 terrorist attacks was released, and it included the number of people who had perished: 2,830. Now Carter had no doubt that she had been given a warning about the terrorist attacks before they happened. If she was right, she had a gift that was as powerful as it was unexplainable.

Mind Power

People such as Carter, who are able to peer into the future and see things before they happen, are said to have a skill known as precognition, or premonition, which is one type of extra-sensory perception (ESP). A phenomenon that is as controversial as it is mysterious, ESP is sometimes called the sixth sense, the paranormal, psychic powers, or just "psi." Whatever it is called, ESP is most easily defined as the ability to perform tasks outside the normal human senses by tapping into the power of the human mind.

Sally Rhine Feather is one of the world's best-known specialists in the field of ESP. Following in the footsteps of her father, ESP pioneer Joseph Banks "J.B." Rhine, Feather devotes her professional career to the study of psychic phenomena. She is a psychologist as well as a parapsychologist, or someone who has been professionally trained in the scientific study of psychic powers. Feather is the person the Carters contacted when they wanted to talk about what had happened. After meeting with them, she believed that Becky Carter possessed the gift of ESP.

A Controversial Science

Feather has heard thousands of stories like Carter's, and like her famous father, she has no doubt about the existence of ESP. But because it is such a mysterious phenomenon, as well as difficult to prove within the parameters of conventional science, many people are skeptical about it. Humans tend to believe only what they can see, hear, touch, taste, and smell with their senses, and ESP involves powers that are outside those senses. With all the mystery and uncertainty surrounding it, people often dismiss

"John, something's going to happen,"
—Becky Carter said to her husband on September 4, 2001, only days before the terrorist attacks.

A man correctly predicts which Zener card a researcher is holding. Although many acknowledge its existence, ESP is difficult to prove within the parameters of conventional science.

ESP as nonsense or hocus-pocus. But to those who say they have experienced the phenomenon for themselves, it is a very real indication of the untapped potential of the human mind.

Brian D. Josephson terms the dismissal of psychic phenomena *pathological disbelief*. Josephson is a scientist and a former winner of the Nobel Prize in physics. He says that when his peers reject the notion of telepathy and other paranormal powers, they are no different from the scientists of the past who scoffed at new theories and ideas. He cites the example of geologist Alfred Wegener, who published his theory about continental drift in 1915 and was the object of ridicule, scorn, and even hostility for many years. Not until after Wegener's death did the scientific world admit that his theory was logical and likely correct. Josephson gets frustrated by this rejection of new ideas that are outside of the established way of thinking, as he explains:

> The statement "even if it were true I wouldn't believe it" seems to sum up this attitude. . . . Science is often presented as an objective pursuit, but the history of science tells you that this is far from being the case. . . . It's also hard to change how people think. People have vested interests, and their projects and reputations would be threatened if certain things were shown to be true.[2]

For Josephson and the many others who believe strongly in extrasensory perception, there is no doubt that "certain things" are, in fact, true. For the scientists who are most skeptical, however, the whole notion of ESP is foolishness.

"It's . . . hard to change how people think. People have vested interests, and their projects and reputations would be threatened if certain things were shown to be true."

—Scientist Brian D. Josephson expressing his frustration with his peers who reject the notion of paranormal powers.

CHAPTER 1

The Roots of ESP

People throughout the world have long believed in the unexplainable powers of the human mind. In ancient times mediums were often consulted when people wanted to communicate with the spirits of their dead ancestors. Before the mediums made contact with the spirit world (known as channeling), they went into a trance, or hypnotized themselves. That ability alone caused people to be in awe of them, and even to fear them.

Mediumship was found in many ancient cultures. The Chinese, for instance, were communicating with the spirit world 4,000 years ago, and in Japan there are records of mediumship that trace back to the eighth century A.D. Channeling was also customary in other countries, including Korea, South America, Finland, Egypt, and Greece.

According to paranormal researcher Michael Schmicker, mediums in ancient times used a number of methods to help them

achieve a trancelike state. He explains: "In addition to . . . tools like Ouija boards . . . mediums used a variety of herbs, drinks and potions, drugs, rituals, prayers and mental and physical exercises to put themselves in a special state of consciousness or trance possession that allowed direct mental contact with the spirit world."[3]

Religious Influence

These mysterious spiritual encounters were common until monotheistic religions, or those that recognize only one deity or god,

Some mediums use Ouija boards (pictured above) as a way to communicate with the deceased and spirit world.

became the center of spiritual life for people in Europe and other parts of the world. Judaism and Islam were the prominent monotheistic religions until the Middle Ages, and then Christianity began to spread and grow more powerful. Although these religions were very different from each other, what they shared in common (in addition to monotheism) was their recognition of prophets, or people with special powers that allowed them to predict the future. Their prophecies were clearly examples of spiritual channeling, but they were considered acceptable because they revolved around religion. The Bible, for instance, tells how the prophets Moses, Jeremiah, and John the Baptist experienced divine inspiration and shared the word of God with others. The same is true of the Koran, the holy book of the Muslims who practice Islam. In the early seventh century A.D., the prophet Muhammad described in the Koran visions he had received from Allah, the deity whom he referred to as the Lord.

The more powerful and widespread monotheistic religions became, the more people were expected to adhere to their strict teachings and rules. Christianity strongly frowned on spirit communications, as did Islam, and religious leaders sought to control and suppress any views of the afterlife that were in conflict with the Koran or the Bible. Anyone who claimed to have channeling powers outside of religion was taking a grave risk and could be severely punished, as Schmicker explains:

> The church wanted to be the only medium authorized to pass on messages from God. But even [communicating with deceased relatives] could put you in jeopardy: if discovered, you could still be accused of communicating with the Devil or

evil spirits. Worse yet, a channeler discovered in a trance . . . risked being accused of being possessed by an evil spirit. And the penalty could be death.[4]

During the late seventeenth and early eighteenth centuries, monotheism started to lose its strength and dominance. This period in history was first known as the Age of Reason and was later called the Age of Enlightenment. It was a time when scientists, philosophers, and other intellectual thinkers began to publicly challenge the existence of God and other deities, and they scoffed at the notion of life after death or anything else that was related to the spirit world. Armed with logic, objective reasoning, and sound scientific principles, the scientists attacked established beliefs and ridiculed anyone who looked to religion or divine spirits for answers about life or death. Their message influenced many people to become more skeptical about religion—but it also paved the way for a different kind of movement that focused on the afterlife and communication with the spirit world.

The Spiritualist Era

That movement, which began in the mid-nineteenth century, was known as Spiritualism. For centuries organized religions had quelled people's freedom to communicate with the afterlife, but Spiritualism seemed to cancel out those restrictions. The result was a powerful revival of interest in channeling, as author and parapsychology expert Jon Klimo explains: "Just as the banning of a book may only lead more people to seek it out, so the vehement opposition to mediumship by traditional organized religion, and by the majority of the press, academia, and scientists

Most researchers believe that Spiritualism started with two sisters from Hydesville, New York, named Kate and Margaret "Maggie" Fox. In March 1848 the girls and their parents reportedly heard strange sounds in their farmhouse, including rapping, or knocking, and what sounded like furniture being moved. The sounds continued over the following days, and the Fox sisters

This illustration of a Ouija board is another example of tools used by some mediums to contact the dead.

of the day, meant that many others were led toward, not turned away from, the phenomenon."[5]

claimed that they were able to communicate with the spirit that was making the noise. They said it was a peddler named Charles B. Rosma, who had been murdered years before and who was buried beneath the house. Even when the girls left their home and traveled to different locations, the noises reappeared wherever they were. Word spread quickly of the young mediums from New York who were somehow tapped into the spirit world. Before long, the channeling craze caught on, and other people started claiming that they, too, had mystical powers. Séances, which were gatherings where these alleged mediums called forth spirits of the dead, became all the rage.

By 1849 the Fox sisters were among the most famous mediums in the world. People traveled great distances to see them and gladly paid admission to attend séances where the girls displayed their skills. These were elaborate affairs, during which Maggie and Kate conveyed messages from the spirit world through taps and knocks, written messages from spirits (known as automatic writing), and voice communication. The sisters developed a huge following of fans, including many prominent, well-known citizens such as authors James Fenimore Cooper and William Cullen Bryant, New York Supreme Court justice John Worth Edmunds, and Wisconsin governor Nathaniel Tallmadge. Another firm believer in the Fox sisters' power was Horace Greeley, editor of the *New York Tribune*. Greeley invited the girls to stay at his home, and after watching them demonstrate their powers on a number of occasions, he was inspired to write about them in his newspaper. He made it clear to readers that he had no doubts about their powers. "Whatever may be the origin or cause of the 'rappings,'" he wrote, "the ladies in whose presence they occur do not make them. We tested this thoroughly and to our entire satisfaction."[6]

As the Fox sisters' fame continued to grow, the grueling demand of being celebrities began to take its toll on them. They were constantly sought out by awestruck crowds of people, and their séances drew massive publicity. Some newspaper articles praised their skills as amazing feats, but others were harshly critical and accused the young women of faking their psychic abilities to deliberately trick their audiences. There were also examiners who attended the séances for the sole purpose of testing the Fox sisters' powers. Their goal was to prove the sisters were fooling people by creating the knocking sounds themselves, perhaps by snapping their joints. In spite of these efforts to discredit them, no one ever actually proved that fakery was involved, but some people still insisted that the sisters were frauds. Eventually the pressure was too much, and both Maggie and Kate began to abuse alcohol. By the early 1880s the Fox sisters, who had once been famous celebrities, had gained the reputation of being drunks, and people were no longer interested in them.

Psychic Investigations

Spiritualism, however, did not lose its intrigue. The movement's popularity was still growing, and it had even caught the attention of a few scientists who were curious enough to investigate it. One of these scientists was a world-famous British physicist and chemist named Sir William Crookes. When the Spiritualism movement had first started, he was highly skeptical, believing that it was just an example of superstition and trickery. But as a scientist, he felt that it was his duty to examine any mysterious phenomena, rather than just discarding new theories without considering whether they might be genuine. Having no idea what he might discover, Crookes decided to start investigating people who claimed to

In this illustration psychic researcher William Crookes holds up a phosphorus lamp to illuminate a spirit. He became know as the leading scientific investigator of spiritualistic phenomena.

The Roots of ESP

The Scientist, the Medium, and Katie King

One of the most famous ESP mysteries of all time involved Florence Cook, who was known as one of the greatest mediums who ever lived. When Cook was a teenager during the 1870s, witnesses said that a spirit named Katie King came out of her body during séances. But because other people accused her of being a fake, Cook invited world-famous British scientist Sir William Crookes to investigate her. For three years Crookes attended séances and studied Cook in his laboratory. After reportedly seeing and photographing the spirit numerous times, he swore that

have psychic powers. Before long, he was known as the leading scientific investigator of Spiritualistic phenomena.

One of the people Crookes investigated was Daniel D. Home, another world-renowned medium who had earned his fame by demonstrating channeling and clairvoyance powers that left people feeling stunned. In one of his séances at the home of a wealthy businessman from Connecticut, witnesses reported that

Cook was telling the truth. Skeptics, however, scoffed at him. They accused him of having a love affair with Cook and lying to hide his romantic involvement with her. In a biography titled *The Medium and the Scientist*, author Trevor Hall denounces both Crookes and Cook. "The weight of evidence appears to show that Florence Cook's mediumship was shamelessly fraudulent," Hall writes. "Once this is accepted, then the conclusion that William Crookes became her accomplice seems inescapable." To this day, there are people who firmly believe that Cook's powers were authentic—and just as many others who believe her only power was an uncanny ability to fool her audiences.

Quoted in Jon Klimo, *Channeling: Investigations on Receiving Information from Paranormal Sources.* New York: St. Martin's, p. 103.

they watched Home levitate, or rise from the floor, and float all the way up to the ceiling. On other occasions he reportedly made an accordion play without his fingers anywhere near the keys. From the very beginning, Crookes was suspicious of Home, so he took extra precautions to keep the man from cheating. For the musical test, Crookes purchased a new accordion and custom-built a wire cage and then hosted a séance at his own house. He placed

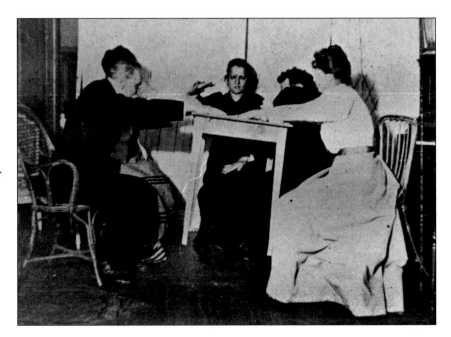

Psychic Eusapia Palladino (center) performs a table levitation. Palladino was observed and studied by researchers from the Society for Psychical Research around 1890.

the accordion inside the cage and pushed the cage underneath a table. As nine witnesses watched closely, Home sat at the table, resting one hand on it, and with his other hand reached into the cage to touch the accordion on the end opposite the keys. The instrument began to expand and contract, playing a simple melody. Then Home removed his hand from the accordion and placed it on the hand of a person sitting next to him—and the instrument still continued to play.

At a different séance, Home impressed Crookes with his levitation powers. Crookes said he had watched with his own eyes as Home rose into the air, and he knew there was no trickery involved because he participated in the demonstration. Crookes explained, "When he rose 18 inches [46cm] off the ground I passed my hands under his feet, round him, and over his head when he was in the air."[7]

When Crookes had first begun to investigate psychic phenomena, his fellow scientists were confident that he would pronounce Spiritualism to be a hoax and expose mediums such as Home to be frauds. But much to their dismay, that did not happen. Instead, Crookes expressed his opinion, verbally and in writing, that psychic phenomena did exist—and by doing so, he angered the scientific community. It denounced Crookes as a scientist and ridiculed his investigative conclusions. Yet despite the hostility that was directed toward him, Crookes would not waver from his position that there were people who possessed mysterious psychic powers.

The Society for Psychical Research

Although Crookes's steadfast belief in Spiritualism caused many scientists to reject him, there were a number of other prominent people who supported him and sympathized with his plight. Two of his supporters were noted British philosophers Henry Sidgwick and Frederic Myers, both of whom shared Crookes's curiosity about the unknown. In 1882 Sidgwick and Myers formed the Society for Psychical Research (SPR), a group dedicated to investigating psychic phenomena. The SPR's mission was to use the principles of science to examine claims of mediumship, clairvoyance, and telepathy. Within a decade the organization grew to more than 1,000 members as scientists, philosophers, and other curious intellectual thinkers decided to join. Crookes eventually became a member, as did British scientist Oliver Lodge and noted psychologists Sigmund Freud and Carl Jung. Not all the group's members believed in psychic phenomena, and some were openly skeptical. But the founders of the SPR welcomed anyone who was interested in participating in their studies, no matter what he or she believed.

The Society for Psychical Research interested researchers from different backgrounds and fields, including famous Austrian psychiatrist Sigmund Freud.

In 1885 the American branch of the Society for Psychical Research was founded by a psychologist and philosopher from Harvard University named William James. As with the British group, a number of distinguished citizens became members of the American SPR, including President Theodore Roosevelt, astronomer and mathematician Simon Newcomb, attorney Clarence Darrow, and author Samuel Clemens, better known as Mark Twain.

Over the following years, the British and American branches of the SPR investigated a number of people who claimed to be mediums. Some, such as Leonora Piper from Boston, appeared to have real psychic powers for which there was no scientific explanation. Piper was a well-known medium who had impressed James and his colleagues with her channeling skills, and the SPR appointed noted psychical researcher Richard Hodgson to investigate her. After attending more than 50 séances, the normally skeptical Hodgson concluded that Piper did indeed have the ability to communicate with the spiritual world. He publicly stated that she displayed abilities while in a trancelike state that "could not be accounted for except on the hypothesis that she had some supernormal power."[8]

Many SPR members agreed that Piper had psychical powers, but that was not the case with most of the mediums they investigated. Too many of them were proven to be frauds, and this was a source of embarrassment for the SPR. Members began to spend the majority of their time working to expose people who falsely claimed to have channeling abilities. Then, in 1888, the group was dealt a major blow. Maggie Fox appeared on a New York stage and, in front of several thousand people, confessed that she and her sister had faked their psychic demonstrations. Skeptics whooped with joy because the confession proved what they had thought all along: The Fox sisters, as well as the entire Spiritualism movement, were nothing but hoaxes. But the diehard Spiritualists refused to believe that Fox was telling the truth. They were convinced that years of alcoholism, combined with abuse and ridicule by critics, had broken her spirit. Even when she later admitted that her confession had been a lie, the damage was already done. The entire Spiritualism movement was being questioned, and the SPR's credibility had been damaged.

By the early twentieth century, interest in Spiritualism had begun to die out. Too many mediums had been exposed as frauds, which meant that anyone claiming to have channeling powers was also assumed to be fraudulent. Psychic researchers knew that their reputations were at stake, and drastic changes were needed. Schmicker explains, "They had no choice—if they wanted respect instead of scorn, they had to leave the séance parlor."[9]

The Father of Parapsychology

But even though many people had lost faith in Spiritualism, there were still numerous others who continued to believe in it, including a group of noted psychologists, professors, scientists, and

"A channeler [in the seventh century A.D.] discovered in a trance . . . risked being accused of being possessed by an evil spirit. And the penalty could be death."

—According to paranormal researcher Michael Schmiker.

Zener cards, shown here, are special cards used for testing for telepathic clairvoyance skills.

other respected professionals. One scientist who was particularly interested in the powers of the human mind was J.B. Rhine. During the early 1920s, when he was working on his doctoral degree at the University of Chicago, Rhine attended a lecture on psychical research that was given by Sir Arthur Conan Doyle. An internationally known author and creator of the famous fictional detective Sherlock Holmes, Doyle was a staunch and outspoken believer in the spirit world and life after death. After hearing him speak, Rhine was fascinated as well as inspired—so much so that he decided to abandon his plans to pursue a career in botany and instead focused on psychical research.

After studying at Harvard for several years, Rhine transferred to Duke University in 1928. There, Rhine coined the terms *parapsychology* and *extrasensory perception* in order to formalize a new scientific discipline for the study of psychic phenomena. He believed the names would help him avoid the negative connotations of séances, ghostly beings, and circuslike hoopla that had become so entwined with the Spiritualism movement. Sally Rhine Feather explains, "My father . . . was a pioneer in applying this necessary scientific approach to a phenomenon previously considered mere superstition or folklore at best. He is credited with bringing the whole topic of the psychic or paranormal out of the séance room and into the research laboratory and to scientific respectability."[10] In the early 1930s Rhine and his wife, Louisa, established the Duke Parapsychology Laboratory, the world's first academic setting for parapsychology research.

From Research to Experimental Science

Rhine had originally planned to focus on studies that could prove or disprove life after death. One of the first people he met with was a British woman named Eileen Garrett, who was known worldwide as a skilled medium. Garrett's channeling skills had made her famous, but she found her strange, supernatural powers to be puzzling. She had no control over them; they came to her spontaneously, and she wanted to find a scientific answer that could explain them. She had willingly submitted to testing in England, so when the American SPR invited her to participate in scientific testing with Rhine, she gladly agreed. When she met with him, she explained her desire to know what forces were taking control of her body and voice when she was in a trance. She wondered whether it was really spirits or possibly just her unconscious mind at work. But even though Rhine believed that Garrett had channeling abilities, he determined that it was not possible for scientific tests to answer her questions with any certainty.

Rhine decided to shift his focus from channeling to two other types of ESP: telepathy (mind reading) and clairvoyance. From his years of research, he knew there were people who claimed to have telepathic powers that allowed them to gain information about the thoughts, feelings, and activities of others by communicating only through the mind. He knew of other people who claimed clairvoyant powers, or the power to see events in clear detail as they actually happened, even in distant or hidden locations.

Rhine used college psychology students as his volunteers, or subjects, and he performed experiments with special decks of cards known as Zener cards. Each deck had 25 white cards that were printed with simple, distinct patterns: a circle, a plus sign, a hollow square, a star, and 3 vertical wavy lines. There were 5 cards of each pattern in a deck, so anyone being tested had a 1-in-5 chance of correctly guessing a particular card's pattern. For the telepathy tests, 1 subject (the sender) shuffled the deck and placed it face down on the table. Then he or she looked at a card and concentrated on the symbol printed on it; meanwhile, a second subject (the receiver) tried to determine what symbol was on the card by reading the sender's mind. Zener cards were also used for clairvoyance tests, but the experiments involved only one subject rather than 2. A dealer shuffled the cards and laid them face down on the table, and then a subject tried to predict what each card was without seeing it. As the experiments were completed, the scores were recorded and tallied. Higher scores suggested a greater probability that a subject possessed ESP powers rather than was merely making lucky guesses.

Rhine was encouraged by the test results. With some of the experiments, the probability of achieving the same results by chance alone was less than 1 in 1 million. But a later clairvoyance experiment had such amazing results that he described it as "the most phenomenal thing that I have ever observed."[11] A subject named Hubert Pearce succeeded in correctly guessing all 25 cards in a row—and the odds against that happening were 1 in 300 quadrillion.

Over the next 30 years, Rhine performed hundreds of these and other controlled lab experiments. Although many of the tests had successful, even astonishing results, that was not true every time. Scientists monitored his progress with interest, and

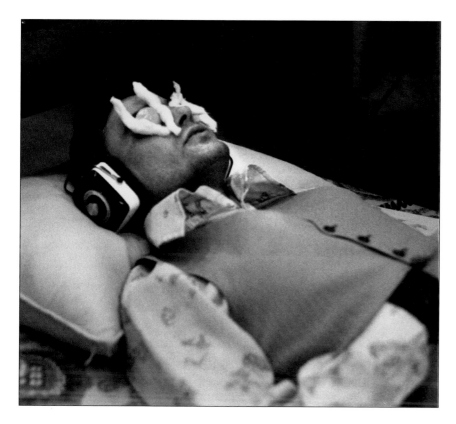

The Rhine Research Center uses a method called the Ganzfeld technique in its studies. The idea is for the subject to be coaxed into a relaxed state of consciousness by eliminating all distractions. Once in this state, Rhine believes the subject is more likely to experience psychic activity.

those who were most skeptical about parapsychology criticized Rhine for never finding an exact answer for how, when, or why ESP powers operated. "For all his research," writes Schmicker, "ESP remained a quirky, paranormal phenomenon. In the end, however, even though his findings violated many laws of classical physics, Rhine believed he had collected enough solid, scientific evidence to prove to any open-minded person the reality of ESP."[12] A number of scientists, psychologists, and other professionals agreed with him. Others, however, openly stated that they would never acknowledge the possibility of ESP because its existence could not be proven with absolute certainty.

CHAPTER 2

Strange and Unexplained

In 1898 an American author named Morgan Robertson published a short novel called *Futility*. It was the story of *Titan*, a British ship that was said to be the biggest, most luxurious vessel ever built. In Robertson's words, *Titan* is "the largest craft afloat and the greatest of the works of man." The ship is 800 feet (20m) long, weighs 45,000 tons (40,823t), and has the capacity for up to 3,000 passengers. The fictitious ship, which is compared to a "first-class hotel," has two brass bands, two orchestras, and a theatrical company to entertain guests as well as numerous other amenities that cater to wealthy travelers. "In short," Robertson writes, "she was a floating city—containing within her steel walls all that tends to minimize the dangers and discomforts of the Atlantic voyage—all that makes life enjoyable."[13] *Futility*'s story takes place during the month of April, when the ship is on its third voyage, sailing from America to Europe.

Titan is said to be unsinkable as well as indestructible—but as the book's tragic conclusion shows, neither prove to be true. One evening around midnight, when *Titan* is a few hundred miles off the American coast, it crashes into an iceberg on its starboard (right) side and sinks into the deep, cold waters of the North Atlantic. There are not enough lifeboats for all the passengers, and nearly 3,000 people die when the ship goes down.

Precognition or Coincidence?

Futility, of course, was not a true story; it was only a product of the author's imagination. The son of a Great Lakes ship captain, Robertson had become a sailor himself and then later began writing stories about the sea. When he wrote *Futility* in 1898, there were many ships traveling through the North Atlantic, but none of them even came close to resembling the enormous luxury passenger vessel that he described. Yet 14 years after his book was

In 1898 an American author named Morgan Robertson published a short novel titled Futility, *about a ship named* Titan. *The story was so similar to the fate of the* Titanic *(pictured) that some believed Robertson had a premonition.*

published, a real-life disaster made some people wonder whether Robertson had peered into the future before he wrote it.

In April 1912 a massive British luxury liner was on its maiden voyage from Europe to New York. The ship's name, the *Titanic*, was nearly identical to Robertson's fictitious *Titan*. But there were far more similarities between the two ships than just their names. Both of the vessels were sailing through the North Atlantic during the month of April, and they were almost identical in size and weight. Like the ship in *Futility*, the *Titanic* was an ocean liner that was like nothing that had ever been built before. It, too, was said to be indestructible and unsinkable, but like *Titan*, it was not. On the night of April 15, the *Titanic* struck an iceberg on its starboard side when it was about 400 miles (645km) off the coast of North America. Water began rushing into the ship, and less than three hours later it snapped in two and sank to the bottom of the sea. Because there were not enough lifeboats onboard to carry all the ship's passengers, more than 1,500 people died, either by drowning or by freezing to death in the icy ocean water.

In spite of the many things *Futility* and the real-life *Titanic* disaster had in common, many people refused to believe that Robertson had a vision of the future when he wrote his book. One of the doubters was author and scientist Martin Gardner, who wrote a book called *The Wreck of the Titanic Foretold?* Gardner, a well-known skeptic of ESP, dismissed the possibility of precognition and wrote that the similarities were nothing more than coincidence. In his book Gardner includes excerpts from a novel by a British journalist, a short story called "The White Ghost of Disaster," and several poems about ships that sink after they hit icebergs in the North Atlantic. He used the passages to illustrate how easy it can be to find connections between incidents if one looks for them. "In most cases of startling coincidences," he writes, "it is impossible to make even a rough estimate of their probability."[14] *New York Times* journalist John Gross challenged Gardner's refusal to even consider that a connection might be possible. In an article about Gardner's book, Gross reminds readers that the author was not only a writer of science and mathematics but also someone who was well known for denouncing believers in psychic phenomena.

But Gardner was not the only person who publicly challenged the idea of Robertson's psychic vision. In the same way that certain people scoffed at the existence of ESP, they also felt that drawing parallels between the fictitious *Titan* and the *Titanic* was foolishness. Senan Molony, an author who specializes in writing about the *Titanic*, was highly skeptical. In an online article for the Titanic Book Site, Molony brought up another possibility for Robertson's "vision" that had nothing to do with coincidence: Years before *Futility* was ever published, three different ships named *Titania* capsized and sank in the North Atlantic—and at least one of the disasters was caused by an iceberg. "So was Morgan Robertson a prophet?" asks Molony. "Or did he just profit from a litany of ill-luck?"[15]

Russia's Most Famous "Psychic"

The dispute over Robertson's alleged vision is not unlike the controversy that has long surrounded all psychic phenomena. People who are skeptical about ESP believe that any account of unexplained powers is fodder for ridicule. One example of a controversial ESP story involves Wolfgang Messing, a Jewish man who was born in 1899 in Poland. Even now, accounts of Messing's psychic abilities are debated among scientists and academicians because much of what is known about him has been obtained from his own autobiographical writings. One person who knew him, Alexander Golbin, was convinced that Messing was gifted with psychic abilities. Golbin, a scientist and child psychiatrist, became acquainted with Messing when they both lived in the Soviet Union. Golbin experienced the man's amazing powers when he made numerous predictions about Golbin's future. Messing, for example, said that Golbin would one day become a doctor, and he also told Golbin that he needed to seriously study the English language. At the time, Golbin found the predictions unbelievable. But in the following years, he did become a doctor, and learning English proved to be invaluable when he was forced to emigrate from Russia and move to the United States.

As controversial as his story is, Messing has been called one of the most convincing psychics who ever lived. In his autobiographical writings, he describes how he ran away from home at the age of 11 and rode the train to Berlin, Germany. During the trip something happened that made him wonder if he had telepathic powers. When a train official walked toward him to collect his ticket, the young passenger was filled with terror because he had no ticket. He knew that people caught trying to ride trains without paying could be severely punished. Messing reportedly handed the official a piece of newspaper and then concentrated hard, envisioning the paper as a ticket. To his amazement, the official hole-punched the paper and then moved on to the next passenger. Messing wondered: Had the man just pitied him for not having a ticket? Or was there another reason he took the newspaper without questioning it?

When Messing was in Berlin, he reportedly amazed people

with his psychic abilities. He found that he could "hear" people's thoughts as though they were speaking out loud, when in fact they were silent. During one of his psychic demonstrations, Messing was said to have correctly predicted the exact day, month, and year that World War II would begin. He also predicted the eventual death of the German dictator Adolf Hitler—and when Hitler heard about it, he ordered that the young man be captured and killed. In fear for his life, Messing fled from Germany to the Soviet Union.

Upon his arrival, Messing was immediately taken into custody by officers of the Soviet secret police organization, the NKVD (later called the KGB). He was turned over to Lavrenty Beria, the head of the organization, for questioning. Before long he was summoned by the Soviet Communist leader Joseph Stalin, who had heard about Messing's alleged psychic powers and wanted to know more. Stalin was determined to find out if Messing's powers were real, so he gave him an ultimatum: either prove that he was not faking it, or be arrested and killed for being a spy. Messing's first test was to find a way to get out of a heavily guarded country house without a pass; Messing said he did that by using telepathy to make the guards think he was Beria. Yet even though Messing had successfully met that challenge, Stalin was not finished with him; in fact, he issued an even tougher challenge. Messing was ordered to go to a bank and leave with 100,000 rubles ($3,800). As NKVD guards stood by and watched, he walked in the bank and handed the teller a plain piece of paper. Without hesitation, the teller gave him the money, and Messing took it and walked out of the bank. Then he went back inside the bank and handed the money over to the teller, who was so shocked at what he had done that he collapsed on the floor. With the guards as his

A Psychic Experience

In May 2006 scientist and parapsychologist Dean Radin received a letter from Ross Hendry, a bookshop owner whose wife had died of cancer. Hendry was filled with grief and desperately wanted to contact her. One night he started to visualize his wife and ask her questions. He believed she was answering him, but he was not sure, so he asked her to give him proof. An "inner voice" told him to go to "Page 4," and when he asked, "Page 4 of what?" the voice said, *"Entangled Minds."* Hendry had purchased Radin's book, *Entangled Minds*, but he had not read it yet. He turned to the fourth page of the book. When he saw the short

witnesses, Messing returned to Stalin's home and told him what he had done. Finally the Soviet leader was convinced, and he allowed Messing to remain in the country.

Based on his personal experience with Messing, Golbin says the man was unique as well as genuine, with talent that deserved respect and admiration. Thirty years after Messing's death in poem printed there, he knew it was a message from his wife. Hendry explains:

> Freda had never even seen or known of the book, and I had never read it. Page 4 does not bear the number 4 so it is not possible that I have had peripheral or unconscious vision of the poem and page number while handling the book. Every other page ... is dense with text that would have been difficult to yield a meaningful response to my question. I knew then with certainty and joy that I was indeed communicating with her.

Quoted in Dean Radin, "A Poignant Psychic Experience," Entangled Minds: Dean Radin's Blog, May 19, 2006. http://deanradin.blogspot.com.

1974, Golbin wrote an article about him titled "A Tribute to the Most Mystic Figure of the 20th Century—the Unusual Mind and Unusual Talent of Wolf Messing." At the end of the article, Golbin explains why he wrote it: "This story is my small payment to his memory and a reminder to scientists that the full abilities of the human mind remain yet to be uncovered."[16]

"It Almost Knocked Me Over"

Like Golbin, Dana Landers (not her real name) also believes in the powers of the human mind, although she did not always feel that way. In 1990 Landers had a personal experience with clairvoyance that she found startling as well as unsettling. Until that point in her life, Landers had called herself "one of the world's biggest skeptics" about ESP. But after hearing many stories from her friend about an amazing psychic named Olga, Landers decided to go see the woman herself. She did not hope to gain anything from the experience; she just wanted to satisfy her curiosity and prove her friend wrong.

During her meeting with Olga, Landers was mildly impressed by some of the things the woman seemed to know about her past, her family, and her job. But as skeptical as Landers was, she thought they were simply lucky guesses. Then, as she was getting ready to leave, something happened that surprised her. "I was just walking out the door," she says,

> and Olga called after me, "Dana, one more thing—your friend has just bought a house and he is planning to take out the arches above the upstairs windows. You must tell him not to do that because good spirits live there. . . . Please tell him to leave the arches where they are. He will be glad." I said sure, I'd tell him, and then I left, thinking she was just a little bit nuts. I didn't know anyone who'd just bought a house and "good spirits"? Who believes in that kind of stuff anyway?[17]

Landers drove back to work, and as she was walking past her boss's office, she could hear him talking on the phone—and what he was saying shocked her. She recalls:

> The first thing I heard him say was that he had closed the deal on a new house, which was news to me since he hadn't mentioned it before. But when he said, "Yeah, it's an awesome place but as soon as we move in those ugly arches have got to go," it almost knocked me over. Up until that time I thought ESP was just something that crazy people believed in, and if I hadn't gone through this, I'd probably still feel that way. Never again.[18]

Messages from the Other Side

Becky Vollink, a young woman from western Michigan, also had a personal experience with a psychic. In May 2001 Vollink's husband died unexpectedly at the age of 27, leaving her alone to raise a 2-year-old daughter and the unborn child she was carrying. She was devastated and felt completely lost without him. About 6 months after his death, she was out for a walk and noticed a small barnlike structure that she had not seen before. There was a sign on the front that advertised the services of a medium named Roslyn, and on a whim, Vollink decided to go inside. She was not prepared for what happened next, as she explains:

> The whole thing was unreal. I walked in the door and told her that something bad had happened to me and I thought she might be able to

help, and she looked at me and said, "Yes, you want to talk to me about your husband Dave because he died." It shocked me so much it knocked the wind out of me—I mean, I'd never seen this woman before in my life, and the second she saw me she knew that my husband had died and what his name was. Not only that, she also said, "You have a two-year-old daughter, don't you?" I told her yes, I did, and she said, "And just about every day you glance at the clock when the time is exactly 11:11—right?" How she knew that I have no idea, but I DID look at the clock at 11:11, sometimes twice a day! Right then I knew this woman might have something that I needed in my life, and I made an appointment to see her again and spend more time with her.[19]

When Vollink went back to see the psychic, she says the woman put herself into a trance and shortly thereafter said she had made contact with Dave's spirit. Vollink recalls:

It was a little creepy at first because her body was shivering and she was talking in a weird voice, so I couldn't help wondering if it was all an act. But when she said that Dave had some things he wanted to tell me, I was just filled with this sense of calm. It was like I felt happy and peaceful for the first time since he had died, and I knew it was because he was there in the room with me. It was such a relief that I almost started to cry.[20]

Vollink says that as Roslyn kept talking, there was no doubt in her mind that Dave was using the medium to communicate with her:

> She said he wanted to thank me for leaving his wedding ring on his finger when he was buried, and that he was glad it comforted me to sleep on the pillow that he used to sleep on—and both of those things were true. She used some funny nicknames he used to call me that ONLY he and I knew about, and she said he missed the times when we used to lie on the couch and talk with our feet pushed together. The last thing she said was that he knew I was hurting and to let me know that I was going to be okay. By the end of the meeting, I felt so much better. It was still hard to go on without him, but somehow knowing that I had found a way to talk to him helped me to heal.[21]

Vollink says she is careful who she tells about the experience:

> When I've told a few people what happened they look at me like I've lost my mind, and I can't really blame them because it does sound far-fetched. I guess the only way anyone can understand is if they experience it for themselves. We're only human after all—who can say there isn't something out there that's beyond what we know and understand? I think it's arrogant of us to assume that. And I can say from personal experience that this was as real as it gets.[22]

Child Psychic

People like Roslyn who claim to have psychic powers often say they became aware of their skills at a very young age. That is true of Sylvia Browne, who says she had her first psychic experience when she was just three years old. One day she surprised her parents by announcing that she was going to have a baby sister. "She'll come in three years—when I'm six," [23] she told them. And sure enough, just one month before Browne's sixth birthday, her sister Sharon was born.

Not all of Browne's visions were happy ones, however. She says a psychic incident that happened when she was five years old was terrifying. She was seated next to her father at a Sunday family gathering when she happened to glance at her great-grandmother—and to her shock and horror, she saw that the woman's face was slowly melting. Browne's biographer and friend, Antoinette May, explains: "Her [great-grandmother's] features were running like wax, slowly oozing downward until there was no face—only a skull."[24] Sylvia screamed in terror, and she was even more frightened when she looked at her other great-grandmother and saw the same thing; her face was also melting. Sylvia began sobbing and begging her father to take her home. Her parents did not take her fears seriously, but within two weeks both of her great-grandmothers died.

Browne tells of another psychic experience that happened a couple of years later. Her father had taken her to a movie and they were having a great time, until she was suddenly overcome with panic. No matter how hard she tried, she could not fight it off. "Am I dying?" she thought wildly. "'No,' a voice inside replied, 'someone else is.'"[25] Then an image flashed into her mind— her baby sister was gasping for air. She told her father they had

to go, that something was wrong with Sharon, that she could not breathe, but he was impatient with her and did not want to leave. Finally he could see that Sylvia was growing more distraught by the second, so he grudgingly agreed to go home. As soon as they pulled into the driveway, Sylvia's mother came running out of the house toward the car. She was sobbing, saying that Sharon was terribly ill and she had not been able to call for help because the phone was out of order. Sylvia's father rushed the baby to the hospital, where she was treated for double pneumonia. If he had not left the movie and gone home when he did, Sharon would have died.

Browne says that in the years since she first discovered her powers, it has not always been easy to live with them. Sometimes the visions are painful, but she has learned to accept whatever comes her way. She has also learned to accept whatever challenges she has been given, and she explains how she views herself and others like her: "Psychics are really just human beings with a gift, which does not serve us personally very well. I have found, as I get older, that the gift is not for my benefit in any way, shape, or form. It is something to be given away. If psychics could benefit from their gift, they would simply win the big lotto and never do what they are supposed to do—help others." [26]

CHAPTER 3

Psychic Detectives

Of all the people who are known for having psychic powers, Noreen Renier is among the most famous. Renier, who refers to herself as a psychic detective, says she has worked on more than 450 cases with law enforcement agencies throughout the United States as well as in six other countries. One of the police officers who has worked with her in the past is retired commander Ray Krolak from Florida. After one particular case, he explained why he has such faith in Renier's psychic abilities: "Noreen never could have known this stuff beforehand and she was so accurate it was chilling."[27]

In February 2003 Renier received a telephone call from Jackie Peterson, a woman who lived in San Diego, California. Peterson's daughter-in-law, Laci, of Modesto, California, was eight months' pregnant and had been missing for more than a month. No one had seen or heard from her since Christmas Eve morning, when

her husband said she had gone out to take the dog for a walk. The family feared that she had been kidnapped, and because the police were not making much progress in the case, Jackie Peterson turned to Renier.

Although Renier preferred to work on cases with the police, she had heard about the Laci Peterson case and was interested in getting involved. She agreed to help and asked Peterson to send her a few of Laci's personal things. She would use the items during her psychic sessions to tap into Laci's energy, or essence, in order to see the world as Laci had.

Connecting with Laci

When Renier received the package, she was disappointed to find that Peterson had sent her only one item, a new sweatshirt that Laci had never even worn. She did not feel that it contained enough energy, so she telephoned Peterson to ask her to send something else. The woman did not answer, and just as Renier

On April 14, 2003, the bodies of a woman and a fetus washed ashore in Richmond, California. They would later be identified as Laci Peterson and her unborn child.

was leaving a message on her answering machine, Laci's husband, Scott Peterson, picked up the phone. She explained who she was and what she needed, and during their brief conversation, she says she became aware of some strong negative feelings. "I told him the problem," she says, "and I could just feel this wall coming down as he talked to me."[28] That was Renier's first indication that something was very wrong.

Scott Peterson sent one of Laci's running shoes to Renier, and even though it was barely worn, she felt that she could move forward. On March 2 and March 24, 2003, she used the items during two different psychic sessions. With her friend transcribing the exact words she spoke, Renier held the personal items close to her body, put herself into a trance, and "became" Laci Peterson—and almost immediately she knew that the young woman had been killed. She said she could feel herself being hit in the head with a bat or some other type of heavy object by an attacker that she knew was a man. She felt her body being placed in a vehicle, concealed with some type of covering, and then driven somewhere for quite a long time. After that she felt herself being submerged in water and weighted down with an anchor that she later said was cement. She said the water surrounding her was more fresh than salty, that there were rocks around her, and lots of fish. She also said, "A bridge is being repaired somewhere and there's a campground or park near the water and the closest road has just been paved."[29]

At the end of each session, Renier sent the transcripts to Jackie Peterson and emailed them to detectives at the Modesto Police Department. A few days after she sent the first email, Modesto police officially declared the Laci Peterson case a homicide, although they did not acknowledge Renier or the information she had provided to them. "The clues were all there," she says, "if the police followed up or not, I don't know. Normally they do."[30]

Renier held a third and final psychic session on March 27, 2003, but this time she did not use the sweatshirt or shoe. Instead, she used only the mailing envelope that Scott Peterson had addressed to her in his handwriting, and she says there was such a strong emission of energy that she felt as if he were in the room with her. During that session Renier assumed the persona of Scott Peterson rather than Laci, and she became certain that he was the killer. The story he had told the police was well publicized—that on December 24, 2002, he had spent the day fishing alone in the San Francisco Bay near the Berkeley Marina, and when he returned home, he found that Laci was missing. Once Renier's psychic visions showed that his story was a lie, she was troubled, as she explains: "I didn't want to see who killed Laci. I knew she was dead when I started on the case, and I didn't really want to see that, but it just sort of popped up right in the beginning, and I sort of pushed it back because I was horrified at what I was seeing, and I didn't want to see that."[31] Renier knew that Jackie Peterson would be angry at what she had learned during her sessions, so when she sent her the final transcript, she omitted any reference to her son's role in the murder. She did, however, email a transcript to the Modesto police that included the information about Scott Peterson.

Horrifying Discoveries

On Sunday, April 13, 2003, the body of a male fetus washed up onto a San Francisco Bay beach a few miles from the area where Scott Peterson said he had been fishing. The next day, the partial torso of a woman was found on the shoreline about a mile away.

The bodies were examined by forensic scientists, and on April 18 they were identified as Laci Peterson and the baby boy whom she had planned to name Conner. That same day Scott Peterson was arrested for murder.

The police investigations revealed similarities between what detectives found and what Renier had seen in her visions and had documented in her transcripts. She had said that Laci Peterson was in an area where there was freshwater, and the San Francisco Bay is part freshwater and part salt water. She had referred to a bridge that was being repaired, and at the time Laci disappeared, the nearby Richmond Bridge was under construction. Renier said that Laci was driven a long way after she was killed, and the area where her body was found was about 90 miles (145km) from her home. Renier believed that Laci was weighted down by cement anchors, and when detectives searched Scott Peterson's home, they found containers of cement and one round cement anchor that he had made. They also found traces of cement in his boat, and on a flatbed trailer he had used, impressions of five round objects were visible in cement dust. Not all of Renier's visions were accurate, however. She had said that Laci was struck on the head with a bat or some other object. Although medical examiners could not tell how she had died, they found no traces of blood or evidence of a struggle, which led them to assume that she had been strangled or smothered.

In November 2004 a jury found Scott Peterson guilty of murdering his wife and unborn son, and he was sentenced to death the following March. Even though Renier's involvement in the case was not acknowledged by the Modesto Police Department, she believes that the information she provided to them was of

value in bringing Peterson to justice. She is aware that many people do not believe she has psychic abilities, and even some say she is nothing but a fraud, but it does not bother her. "The skeptics say, But how does it work? How does it work? And my answer usually to the skeptics is, You use your usual logic, rational thinking mind all the time. Tell me how it works, how you read, how you spell. You can't, and neither can I."[32]

The people who are most skeptical about Renier insist that she did nothing to help solve the Laci Peterson case. They say she merely pulled together a collection of vague information that the police likely found out on their own. One of the most outspoken skeptics is Joe Nickell, an author and investigative columnist for *Skeptical Inquirer* magazine. "No psychic found Laci Peterson," he told a reporter from the *Gainesville (FL) Sun* in May 2003. "I find it astonishing that (Renier's) getting this kind of press coverage, and

Scott Peterson (center) was charged and convicted of murdering his wife. He is currently on death row at San Quentin prison in California.

no one is bringing up her failures." Nickell said that psychics have a trick of throwing out numerous clues early in the case; then once it is solved, they match up vague statements with the actual facts: "They thrive on an uncritical media giving them attention."[33]

Do Police Really Use Psychics?

Nickell acknowledges that some experienced police detectives have used psychics, including a New Jersey police captain who credited the late Dorothy Allison with helping to solve a case. According to Nickell, the captain said that Allison's predictions were difficult to verify when she initially gave them, and their accuracy was not verified until after the investigation was over. Skeptics call this after-the-fact matching, or "retrofitting," and they believe it is the real secret behind most so-called psychic successes. "For example," says Nickell,

> the statement, "I see water and the number seven," would be a safe offering in almost any case. After all the facts are in, it will be unusual if there is not some stream, body of water, or other source that cannot somehow be associated with the case. As to the number seven, that can later be associated with a distance, a highway, the number of people in a search party, part of a license plate number, or any of countless other possible interpretations. Many experienced police officers have fallen for the retrofitting trick.[34]

Many law enforcement professionals share Nickell's views about people who promote themselves as psychic detectives. One

In 2002 Elizabeth Smart (center) was abducted from her home. Investigators received over 1,000 tips from psychics, but no psychic was publicly acknowledged when Smart was found a year later alive.

of the biggest reasons for their skepticism is that so many leads from psychics prove to be incorrect or even deliberate hoaxes. Whenever a major crime occurs, police departments often get hundreds, or even thousands, of calls from people claiming to be psychics. Following up on all those leads wastes time as well as valuable police resources. According to Benjamin Radford, who also writes for *Skeptical Inquirer*, nearly 1,000 psychics contacted the police in 2002 after a teenage girl named Elizabeth Smart was kidnapped from her home in Salt Lake City. Radford says the psychics offered "their visions, information, and evidence," and police followed up on every one of the tips. Smart was found alive a year later, but Radford insists that none of the psychics deserved any credit for it. He says, "Not a single piece of evidence from all those psychics led to the girl's recovery . . . instead Smart's abductors were recognized by two alert couples in a Salt Lake City suburb. News reports, quick thinking, and handy telephones rescued Smart, not psychic powers."[35]

To dispute the many claims by psychics who say they work hand in hand with police to solve tough cases, some law enforcement agencies have publicly denounced the use of psychics. After NBC stated on its Web site that psychic Allison Dubois had assisted numerous law enforcement agencies, including the Texas Rangers, Tom Vinger, a spokesman for the Rangers, flatly denied that it was true: "The Texas Rangers have never used psychics and have no plans to do so."[36]

The Federal Bureau of Investigation (FBI) also denies having any involvement with psychics, and the bureau forbids its agents to use them. In January 2002, however, information that became public made the FBI's denial of using psychics seem questionable. A former lawyer for the U.S. Department of Justice told *New York* magazine that the FBI had reviewed information provided by California psychic Prudence Calabrese, "and in some cases, the information was 'elevated up the channels.'" The lawyer confirmed that the FBI did not use psychics as official sources, but he said there was involvement and it happened "under the table." According to the lawyer, in the aftermath of the terrorist attacks of September 11, 2001, the U.S. attorney general "told us to think outside the box. This is definitely thinking outside the box."[37]

Katherine Ramsland, a well-known author and expert on forensic psychology, says that many people who work in law enforcement do use psychics in their investigations, but they are secretive about it. She explains, "Although skeptics galore decry the use of psychics for anything but entertainment, police departments around the country call on certain psychics when all else fails. They've been doing that for more than a century, and when forbidden to do so, they sometimes use unofficial means."[38]

From Skeptic to Believer

One police officer who is outspoken about his work with a psychic is Fernando Realyvasquez. In 1997, when he was a detective with the police department in Pacifica, California, Realyvasquez was working on the case of Dennis Prado, a former military paratrooper who had vanished without a trace. Prado was reported missing by his sister, who became worried about him when she could not reach him by telephone. The police went to his home and found that his car was still parked there, his wallet and other personal belongings were inside the house, and there was no sign that anything was wrong. Investigators followed up on all leads and clues and assigned rescue teams to search the San Pedro Valley County Park where Prado often hiked. The investigation and search operation continued for more than two months, but the police found nothing. Finally, Prado's family asked Realyvasquez if he would consider talking to a psychic. He had long been skeptical of people who called themselves psychics, and he did not particularly want to work with one, as he explains: "To be honest with you, when they first mentioned that idea to me, I rolled my eyes, just like the next person. . . . I never really have given a psychic's opinion much thought other than, you know, come on. . . . I wasn't really crazy about it, but I thought, OK, let's give it a shot, what do we have to lose?"[39]

Realyvasquez was aware of a psychic named Annette Martin,

and he telephoned her and then went to her office to see her. He showed her a picture of Prado and gave her a large map of the area where the man lived. Martin asked Realyvasquez a number of questions and then concentrated on the photograph. She started saying personal things about Prado: that he loved the color green, that he often wore green clothing, and that he enjoyed going for walks, all of which were true. Martin explains how she began to see him walking in her mind: "I began to track him.... And with the map ... I tracked him out of his condo, down a path and he walked up a path about half a mile or so and turned to the left on this dirt road. And he was heading for this little hill to sit." Suddenly Martin stopped talking and started gasping for air. "I started to feel like I was choking and I couldn't breathe," she says. "And I felt he had fallen over into the brush and I believe had like a heart attack or a stroke."[40] Martin picked up the map, pointed to the San Pedro Valley County Park, and then took a pen and drew a small circle to indicate where Prado could be found. She made it clear that a search dog was going to find him, not a person.

When Realyvasquez saw the place that Martin had circled, he was doubtful. How could she possibly know exactly where he was? The park was enormous, covering more than 2,000 acres (800ha) of land, and the terrain was covered with dense forest, tangled underbrush, and steep cliffs. Moreover, search and rescue teams had been combing the park for weeks and had found no trace of Prado. But Realyvasquez decided he had nothing to lose by checking the area out, so he sent a search team to the park, along with a search dog that had worked with the sheriff's department. Using the map as their guide, team members went to the spot that Martin had circled—and in less than 15 minutes they had found Prado's body exactly where she said it would be. Later, Realyvasquez commented on the role his psychic partner played in the case: "The fact of the matter is that he had been missing for nearly three months. I am still a little bit skeptical, but on the other hand, in this particular case, we probably wouldn't have found him if it hadn't been for Annette Martin."[41]

Psychic Cop

Kathlyn Rhea is another psychic who, like Martin, has earned the admiration of people who work in law enforcement. She has worked on thousands of cases throughout California, helping to solve crimes and find missing persons, and she has proven to be so valuable that two counties, Calaveras and Sonoma, have deputized her. John Crawford, an investigator for the Calaveras County district attorney's office, praises Rhea's abilities: "I heard about her early in my career, and had an open mind, but we've had a lot of people who claim to be psychic who give us information that hasn't panned out. She's been instrumental in composing suspects' pictures that have turned out to be amazingly accurate."[42]

Rhea says her powers are no different from anyone else's—she simply relies on her intuition. But she is more practiced at using it. "If people have five senses then they have six," she says. "It's just that I've been developing mine for 30 years."[43] Rhea says that the reason why most people are not able to use their intuitive powers is because they do not understand them, and cannot accurately interpret them. She spends much of her time teaching people about what she calls "the Three I's": intuition, intellect, and interpretation, which helps them tap into their natural intuitive powers.

The Psychic Who Went to Jail

In 1980 Etta Smith heard a news report about a Los Angeles nurse named Melanie Uribe who had disappeared on her way to work. Smith did not know Uribe, but she was overcome with an urgent feeling that Uribe had been killed and then dumped in a remote canyon. She went to the police department and reported this to detective Lee Ryan, showing him on a map where he could find Uribe's body. Ryan said he would follow up on her tip the next morning, but Smith knew he was skeptical, and she did not believe him. She left the police station and drove to Lopez Canyon. She spotted tire tracks in the dirt and then saw something white in the brush, which turned out to be a pair of nurse's shoes that were still on Uribe's feet. As Smith had envisioned, the woman had been murdered and her body dumped in the canyon. When the police found Uribe's body, they arrested Smith and booked her on suspicion of murder. She spent four days in jail before three men confessed to Uribe's kidnapping and murder. Smith was released, and she promptly sued the police department for wrongful arrest. She won the lawsuit and a cash settlement.

Private investigator Tim McFadden, who worked for 35 years with the Fresno, California, police force, is another of Rhea's admirers. He says that before he met her, he compared the work of psychics to crystal-ball gazing. Then, when he was a police detective working on the case of a missing 10-year-old girl, someone told him he should call Rhea. In spite of his doubts, he took the advice and got in touch with her. Rhea saw visions of feathers, a windmill, and other details, all of which led the police to a field near a chicken ranch—and there they found the little girl's body. According to McFadden, Rhea described the location and the girl's corpse with such accuracy that it gave him chills. "Kay is the real deal,"[44] he says.

"We Don't Always Know Everything"

Whether or not psychics are useful in helping police solve crimes is one of the most hotly debated issues among ESP believers and skeptics. There have been hundreds of situations where police have been totally misled by people claiming to have psychic powers—but there have also been many documented cases where psychics proved to be invaluable. In spite of the controversy, it is a fact that some law enforcement agencies can and do rely on psychics. Janis Amatuzio, a forensic pathologist who directs death investigations for five counties in Minnesota, cautions that police should not rule out the possibility of working with psychics. "I think we don't always know everything yet," she says. "You know, Albert Einstein wrote, 'The most beautiful thing we can experience is the mysterious.' And he made some of the greatest discoveries on earth. So I think it's really important for us to keep that open mind."[45]

CHAPTER 4

Do Animals Have ESP?

In December 2004, when a massive sea wave known as a tsunami struck Southeast Asia, animals seemed to be better prepared than humans. Witnesses reported that shortly before the tsunami pounded the coastlines of eleven countries, creatures of all kinds started behaving strangely. Elephants in coastal areas, including the island countries of Sri Lanka and Sumatra, Indonesia, were seen running away from the beach. At the Elephant Trekking Centre in Khao Lak, Thailand, two elephants started to panic five minutes before the tsunami struck. Trumpeting loudly, they broke free from their chains and ran for higher ground, carrying with them four Japanese tourists who were riding on their backs.

A villager in Bang Koey, Thailand, observed a herd of buffalo grazing by the beach. As scientist and author Rupert Sheldrake reports, before the deadly wave hit, the villager recalled that the

creatures "'suddenly lifted their heads and looked out to sea, ears standing upright.' The buffalo then turned and stampeded up the hill, followed by bewildered villagers, whose lives were saved."[46] At a Sri Lankan wildlife reserve, people reported that a nesting colony of flamingos abandoned low-lying breeding areas and flew to higher ground, which was totally unlike their usual behavior. Tribal groups in the Andaman Islands moved away from the shoreline and fled for higher ground because they were alerted by the way animals behaved. In the aftermath of the disaster, a news photographer flew over Sri Lanka in a helicopter. He could see abundant wildlife, including elephants, buffalo, and deer, but he did not see any animal corpses at all. This was true in numerous areas that were destroyed by the tsunami. In Khao Lak alone, more than 3,000 people lost their lives, but there was not a single animal death.

Hours and minutes before the tsunami of 2004 hit Southeast Asia, people reported that animals acted strangely, suggesting they could sense the coming danger.

How Did They Know?

Throughout history, people have observed that animals seem to sense an impending earthquake or other natural disaster long before humans do. In 373 B.C. historians wrote that huge numbers of rats, snakes, weasels, and other animals deserted the Greek city of Helice just a few days before it was destroyed by a powerful earthquake. Author James M. Deem cites an article that appeared in the 1888 issue of *Nature* magazine stating that "ponies have been known to prance about their stalls, pheasants to scream, and frogs to cease croaking suddenly a little before a shock, as if aware of its coming."[47]

This change in animal behavior prior to a natural disaster has long mystified scientists. Even though they are not sure what causes the changes, the most popular theory is that the creatures' acute senses allow them to hear noises, sniff something unusual in the air, or feel tiny vibrations in the earth that are not detectable by humans.

Sheldrake, however, believes that theory is flawed. He says some animals that respond in advance to earthquakes have senses that are no better than humans. Also, many areas where earthquakes strike are seismically active areas, meaning vibrations in the earth happen frequently. This is especially true in Thailand, Sri Lanka, and other countries that are located in an area known as the Ring of Fire. Every year, an estimated 500,000 detectable earthquakes occur throughout the world. Sheldrake contends, therefore, that if animals were extraordinarily sensitive to weak vibrations, they would often give false alarms or would even have the same response to vibrations that are caused by passing trucks. He believes the real reason animals respond as they do is because they have powers that are not fully understood—

"powers of perception that go beyond the known senses," which not only allow the creatures to sense an impending natural disaster, but also gives them other mysterious abilities. He explains, "Dogs that know when their owners are returning home . . . horses that can find their way home over unfamiliar terrain, cats that anticipate earthquakes—these aspects of animal behavior suggest the existence of forms of perceptiveness that lie beyond present-day scientific understanding."[48]

Animal Premonitions

Whether animals actually do have telepathic powers or "powers of perception" has long been a point of controversy among scientists. What is known, and remains unexplained, is that there have been numerous accounts of animals that acted as though they knew things were going to happen ahead of time. Jeanne Randolph, a woman from Washington, D.C., reported such a story about a cat named Sami that was a present from her boyfriend. Nearly every evening, her boyfriend stopped by her apartment after work. Randolph always knew when he would be there because about ten minutes before he arrived, the cat walked over and sat by the door. She knew she was not giving the cat unconscious signals because her boyfriend worked odd hours, so she never knew when he was coming over. She explains why the cat's behavior was such a mystery to her: "I doubt Sami could have heard his car as I live in the middle of a very noisy city in a high-rise. When my mother visits, she says Sami anticipates my arrival in the same fashion—and I take the subway."[49]

Bryan Roche, who spent a summer on the Massachusetts island of Nantucket, also had an experience with a cat—and he is convinced that it saved him from getting fired from his job.

Roche, who stayed in a guesthouse owned by his employer, shared the residence with a Persian cat named Minu. The cat's owner told Roche that she had a psychic relationship with Minu: About 20 minutes before she arrived home, the cat would always start growling. Roche assumed she was kidding and often joked about it with his friends. Then one night, without the permission of his employer, he hosted a party in the guesthouse. Midway through the evening, he noticed that the cat was acting strangely, arching her back and growling. Even though he doubted that Minu was sending any sort of message, he decided to heed her "warning" and send his guests home. Less than ten minutes later his employer pulled into the driveway. Roche credited the cat with saving his job, and he became curious about her strange abilities. As he observed Minu more closely, he could tell that she was sensing the arrival of her owner no matter what time of the night or day the woman got home, even when she was riding in a different car. Roche explains how he used Minu's mysterious powers to his advantage: "I became so convinced of the reliability of the cat's predictions that I held several more parties to which the cat was cordially invited. On each of these occasions, the cat proved to be a fail-safe employer-arriving alarm."[50]

Protecting People from Harm

In the same way that animals appear to sense people's actions, some have gone out of their way to protect their owners from danger. A woman from Wales named Elizabeth Powell says she received such a warning from her dog, Toby, but at the time she did not pay much attention. One morning when Powell was getting ready to leave the house, Toby went out of his way to stop her from going out the front door. She explains, "He barged against me, leaned on the door, jumped up at me, and pushed me. He is normally a quiet, loving dog and knows my routine; I would have been back within four hours. I had to lock him in the kitchen and left him howling, something he has never done before or since."[51] With Toby contained (although still howling furiously), Powell left her house at 7:30 A.M.—and approximately two hours later she was seriously injured in a traffic accident. She says that in the future she intends to pay attention to Toby's warnings.

Another incident that involved warnings from an animal was reported by a woman in Austria named Franziska Kabusch. On a snowy winter day, Kabusch was driving a horse-drawn sleigh to a nearby village. She had traveled only a short distance when, without warning, the horse stopped and refused to take another step. No matter what she did, the horse refused to move forward; instead, it started walking backward until it splashed into a small stream. Kabusch was growing exasperated at her horse's uncharacteristic stubbornness, but then something happened that made her understand. "Suddenly there was a great thundering noise," she says. "A huge avalanche came down from the roof of the barn in front of us and dropped right onto the part of the road that we were about to use."[52] Sheldrake says it is possible that the horse picked up faint sounds of the avalanche before the massive amount of snow started to slide off the roof—or perhaps the animal was tapping into its precognition powers.

In an article entitled "Animal Psychics?" Deem writes of an incident that took place during the 1930s. William Montgomery had planned to spend the day fishing in the Atlantic Ocean. He got his boat ready to go and then called for his Irish setter, Redsy, who always went along on fishing trips. But that day the dog did not act the same; she stayed on the dock and refused to move, no matter how much Montgomery tried to coax her. Montgomery had no idea what was wrong; it was a lovely, sunny day, with blue skies and just a slight breeze, perfect weather for fishing. But even as he watched other boats heading out into the water, he decided that maybe Redsy sensed something he did not, and he canceled his plans. Less than an hour later, the sky was no longer blue, and the seas were no longer calm. A ferocious hurricane blew in from the sea, bringing with it gale-force winds and 40-foot (12m) waves that pounded the shoreline. More than 600 people died in the storm, including many fishermen who had been out on the water in boats. Fortunately for Montgomery, he was not one of the casualties because he had paid attention to his dog's warning.

Sensing Injury and Death

In addition to alerting people about dangers ahead, some animals have shown signs of knowing that something bad has already happened. Sheldrake experienced this in 1998, when he was watching a dog for some friends. They were on a short vacation in Spain, and their son, Timothy, was on a skiing trip in the Italian Alps. The family's dog, a Labrador named Ruggles, seemed comfortable staying with Sheldrake and spent most of his time lying contentedly in the family room. One morning, however, the dog did not act the same. Sheldrake had taken him out for a walk, and when they returned at 11:30 A.M., Ruggles would not leave the entrance hall; instead, he stayed right by the front door. Sheldrake was puzzled by the dog's changed behavior and wondered if he sensed that his owners had returned home early—but Ruggles had sensed something else. At approximately 11:00 A.M., Timothy had broken his leg after falling off a chairlift and had been airlifted to a hospital in a helicopter. Sheldrake believes that the real reason for Ruggles's changed behavior was some sort of premonition that Timothy had been injured.

Iris Hall, a woman from Oxford, England, had a similar situation with her dog, but her story is far more tragic. Hall's son was in Great Britain's Royal Navy and had been based on land for four years before being assigned to a ship called the *Coventry*. Before he was at sea, he went home to visit his parents as often as he could. The dog was extremely fond of him, and without fail, 20 to 30 minutes before he walked in the door, she excitedly ran back and forth in anticipation of his arrival. One night after her son had shipped out, Hall says, the dog jumped onto her lap, shivering and whimpering, and she had no idea what was wrong. Then on the evening news, she heard that a ship like the one her son was on had sunk. Even though the name was not given, Hall had a terrible feeling it was the *Coventry*, and the next morning she learned that she had been right. The *Coventry* had gone down, and her son was one of the sailors who died. Hall and her husband were devastated by the loss of their son—but they were not the only ones. The dog was so distressed by the loss of her human friend that she herself died a few months later.

An Amazing Journey

Just as scientists are not certain why animals can sense danger and tragedy, they are also not sure how some creatures find their way when they travel. Sometimes animals travel long distances in areas that are totally unfamiliar to them. Nicole and Jay Walsh, who live in the Boston area, experienced this in December 2005 with their dog, Bailey. A few months before, the Walshes had moved across town to a different neighborhood. On a rainy

Did You Know?

Snakes are considered by many experts to be the most sensitive animals to earthquakes.

night in early December, Bailey suddenly darted out the front door and disappeared into the darkness. Jay yelled for the dog to come back, but Bailey did not respond. When Nicole got home from work at midnight, she drove around the neighborhood but saw no sign of the dog. She was scared that he had gotten lost and could not find his way to their new home, or worse, that he had been hurt.

Meanwhile, at a home about 1.5 miles (2.4km) away, Maureen Little heard scratching at her front door. Her dogs, Jesse and Molly, were alert, but they did not bark as they usually did when they heard unusual noises. Maureen and her husband, Chris, peeked out the window and saw standing on their stoop a bedraggled black dog that was soaked from the rain. They told him to go home, but later they heard him scratching at the back door. Chris put an old dog bed outside under an overhang and left food and water for the dog. At about 2:30 in the morning, Maureen woke up and went downstairs. She was astonished to see her dog Molly lying against the sliding glass door on the inside, and the strange black dog lying next to the glass on the outside. Later that morning the rain stopped, and Chris opened the door to let Molly out into the backyard. The 2 dogs ran to each other immediately as though they were old friends. That was when Maureen recognized the black dog. He was one of Jesse's puppies, born 9 years before. She had given all the puppies away except for Molly, and she gave the pick of the litter to her friend from college, Nicole Walsh. It had been at least 5 years since the dogs had seen each other, and somehow—even though Bailey had never made the journey before and was walking through a howling rainstorm—he had miraculously found his way to his mother and sister.

When Nicholas Dodman, who is a scientist and national authority on dog psychology, heard Bailey's story, he said it is "important to realize different animals have different gifts. [Dogs] are almost savants in certain areas. We can only be in awe of their sense of smell." Dodman goes on to explain that dogs have "an acute ability 'to make mental maps.' Whether it's [magnetic] or some other mechanism, a dog can find its way from point a to point b in a pea soup of fog if it really wants to."[53] Unlike Dodman, though, some scientists are not sure that animals' normal senses are the reason they can make seemingly impossible journeys. Instead, they wonder if an animal's ability to accomplish incredible feats is really due to mysterious powers of the mind.

Telepathic Flight?

Animals on the ground are not the only creatures that mysteriously find their way over long distances. The same is true of creatures that travel in the sky. Homing pigeons, for instance, can fly hundreds of miles to find their way back to their lofts. Scientists have been curious about pigeons for years and have studied them extensively. Many believe the creatures are guided by their keen eyesight and ultrasensitive hearing or rely on internal directional compasses. According to Sheldrake, however, that does not explain how pigeons seem to know exactly where they are going when they are flying over unfamiliar terrain or when the ground is not visible because the skies are dark or thick with cloud cover. He says that even if pigeons do have a sort of compass sense, which has not been proven, it does not explain their ability to navigate. "If you were taken blindfolded to an unknown destination and given a compass," he says, "you would know where north was, but not the direction of your

China Listens to Animals

For centuries people in some countries have paid close attention to the behavior of animals in an effort to foresee earthquakes. This has long been true in China, where people in earthquake-prone areas are encouraged to report unusual animal behavior—and while it might be coincidence, the Chinese have a good track record of predicting earthquakes. In late 2006 scientists in Nanning implemented a snake-based earthquake detection system. They use video cameras and 24-hour Internet links to monitor snake nests at local snake farms. According to

home. The failure of conventional attempts to explain pigeon homing and many other kinds of animal navigation implies the existence of a sense of direction as yet unrecognized by institutional science."54

One of the greatest scientific mysteries is the migration of butterflies. Each fall, 100 million or more monarch butterflies leave North America and fly south to winter in the forested mountains experts at Nanning's earthquake bureau, snakes can sense earthquakes from 75 miles (120km) away, three to five days before they strike. The serpents respond by behaving erratically, as Jiang Weisong, the bureau director, explains: "Of all the creatures on the earth, snakes are perhaps the most sensitive to earthquakes. When an earthquake is about to occur, snakes will move out of their nests, even in the cold of winter. If the earthquake is a big one, the snakes will even smash into walls while trying to escape." Jiang says that the system has improved the bureau's ability to forecast earthquakes and could be expanded to other parts of the country.

Quoted in Guan Xiaofeng, "Nanning Turns to Snake-Based System to Predict Quakes," *China Daily*, December 28, 2006. www.chinadaily.com.cn.

of central Mexico. The males die after breeding season in late February, and the female monarchs head back toward the north. After they die, their offspring continue the ongoing cycle. Scientists believe the butterflies have been doing this for thousands of years, and they marvel at the amazing journey. Not only do the fragile, fluttery creatures travel an unbelievable 2,000 miles (3,200km) to reach their destinations, no single butterfly on a journey has experienced it before. Monarch butterflies live for only a few months, so those that travel to Mexico are several generations removed from their ancestors who last left the area. *National Geographic* writer John Roach explains: "Four to five generations separate the monarch populations that make the migration, so the butterflies that make the trek to Mexico are the great, great grandchildren of the previous generation to have made it."[55] Many scientists believe that butterflies make their long journey by relying on internal compasses that are set by the position of the sun in the sky. Others, however, wonder if there are other powers at work that cannot be explained through normal scientific reasoning.

"Your Horse Says You're Lying!"

Bill Northern has no doubt that animals have those types of powers because he says they communicate with him through telepathy. Northern is known as an animal communicator, and he often performs translation services between pets and their owners. Most of his time is spent with horses, but he says he has also worked with dogs and cats. He explains the difference between the animals' attitudes: "Horses look down on us; they think we're around to service them. If you're late bringing their food, a horse thinks, 'what's the matter with that so-and-so?' And dogs think, 'What did I do wrong to deserve a late meal?' Dogs will go out of their way not to hurt your feelings. And cats will think, 'Dinner's late, I better go kill something.'"[56]

As strange as Northern's abilities may seem, he has astounded people who have hired him to help them with their animals. One of his clients, Wayne Shizuru, says Northern is definitely

for real because the things he does are just too amazing to be coincidences. For example, a horse owner told Northern that he was the primary caretaker of the horse, and after hearing what the horse had to say, Northern started laughing. "Your horse says you're lying!" he said. "You're not the main trainer, that guy over there is."[57] He pointed the man out, and the owner admitted he was correct. On a different occasion a horse was suffering from a skin problem. Northern said the animal told him he craved garlic, which sounded silly because horses do not usually eat garlic. But based on what Northern said, Shizuru started feeding the horse a garlic clove every day, and his skin cleared up. There have also been times when horses were misbehaving and Northern helped them resolve their issues. "One of the horses said I called him a [bad name]," says Shizuru, "and his feelings were hurt. Gosh! I did do that several weeks ago while we were out riding, and he acted up, but no one heard me. I apologized and the horse and I are getting along better now."[58]

Northern has faced more than his share of people who doubt him, but he is not bothered by them. "Everyone's a skeptic," he says. "Good! Ten years ago, I was too. I would have committed myself to the funny farm. Since then, I can only tell you what the horses have already told me."[59] According to the many people who have witnessed his work, Northern definitely knows what he is talking about.

Studying ESP

When J.B. Rhine set up the world's first parapsychology laboratory during the 1930s, he had two goals: to perform ESP experiments in a controlled environment and to gain respectability for his work from the scientific community. Most people at that time, especially scientists, believed that the only way ESP's existence could be proven was if quantifiable results could be consistently shown. Because Rhine and others who focused on ESP could not always show the kind of absolute, measurable proof that the skeptics demanded, they were often thought to be frivolous.

Today, although ESP is more widely accepted than it was in the past, many people still do not believe that it exists. According to the Parapsychological Association, one of the main reasons ESP is not universally accepted is because it cannot be successfully tested by repeatable experiments. The organization explains its response to this perspective:

When many people talk about a repeatable psi experiment, they usually have in mind an experiment like those conducted in elementary physics classes to demonstrate the acceleration of gravity, or simple chemical reactions. . . . But insisting

This woman is undergoing a Ganzfeld experiment to test for telepathy.

on this level of repeatability is inappropriate for parapsychology. . . . Psi experiments usually involve many variables, some of which are poorly understood and difficult or impossible to directly control. Under these circumstances, scientists use statistical arguments to demonstrate 'repeatability' instead of the common, but restrictive view that "If it's real, I should be able to do it whenever I want."[60]

Unpredictable Results

One person who publicly insists that repeatable experiments are absolutely necessary to prove the existence of ESP is James Randi, a well-known stage magician who is one of the world's most vocal skeptics of psychic phenomena. Randi is so convinced that ESP is a hoax that his educational foundation offers a $1 million prize to anyone who can prove that he or she has paranormal or supernatural powers in a controlled environment. The list of frequently asked questions on the foundation's Web site explains the likelihood that no one will ever meet the challenge successfully: "While you may be neither mistaken [about having paranormal powers] nor a cheater, the JREF [James Randi Educational Foundation] will always assume that you are one or the other."[61]

Michael Schmicker and other parapsychologists are the first to admit that psychic testing often shows inconsistent results. Yet they reject Randi's belief that all claims of psychic powers "are simply the result of fraud, trickery or sloppy experimental controls."[62] Schmicker acknowledges that there have been numerous occasions when psychics have performed successfully, while at other times they could barely perform at all. He says that kind of inconsistency is to be expected because psychic phenomena are produced by human beings rather than by machines. Psychic performance can be affected by such factors as the knowledge, skills, emotions, health, and beliefs of the person being tested as well as by the testing environment and the attitudes of the people running the tests. Schmicker compares this to sporting events. Professional sports teams typically win more home games than away games because when they are at home, they are playing for a cheering, supportive crowd. According to Schmicker, it is no different with psychics:

> Like a batter in an away game facing a pitcher in a hostile ballpark . . . your performance can be affected by the attitude of people around you. If people want you to fail . . . and radiate hostility, they can usually negatively affect your performance even without physically touching you. For this reason, performing psi feats before a hostile crowd of debunkers is probably harder to do than performing the same feat before a friendly audience, or even a neutral one.[63]

Analyzing Patterns

Schmicker's belief that psychic performance is affected by a number of factors is shared by Sally Rhine Feather and the other professionals at the Rhine Research Center. The organization studies ESP in many different ways, such as collecting and analyzing real-life testimonies from people willing to share their psychic experiences. Louisa Rhine started this practice in 1948, when she began to compile a database of reports she received from all over the world. After reading hundreds of testimonies, Rhine began to see definite patterns among the people's stories, and she could also see that some of their experiences were essentially identical. This, she thought, could be of tremendous value in unlocking the mysteries of ESP and was the key to truly understanding how the human mind works. And while she believed that laboratory experiments served a valuable purpose, she also thought they could "impose artificial constraints on the reality they [tried] to analyze."[64]

Today the Rhine Research Center continues Louisa Rhine's studies with real-life psychic experiences, and the organization has compiled the largest collection of ESP reports in the world. Sally Rhine Feather says this work is significant even though it is not necessarily performed in the lab or a controlled setting. She explains:

> Laboratory experiments are required to prove ESP is real, but ESP usually happens outside the laboratory. Confining our study of ESP to the laboratory is like studying lions in a zoo instead of the wild. To see how lions interact and behave, you have to observe them in their natural habitat. To understand ESP, we have to look at how it manifests itself spontaneously outside the laboratory in daily life.[65]

By studying and analyzing the ESP experiences of ordinary people, Feather and her colleagues have formed a number of conclusions. For instance, they have determined that about 60 percent of psychic experiences happen when people are dreaming. When the visions involve more than one person, they are most common when the people are emotionally or biologically close. Some reports, however, have told of tragic events that affect strangers, such as Becky Carter's premonition about the terrorist attacks. Women reportedly have psychic experiences more often than men, and most visions overwhelmingly relate to negative topics, such as illness, danger, and death.

Telepathy Experiments

Although much of the Rhine Research Center's work focuses on collecting and studying actual psychic experiences, scientists at the organization also perform laboratory experiments. Their goal, according to Feather, is not to prove whether ESP exists— because she says that has already been scientifically established. Instead, she and her colleagues focus on gaining a better understanding of how ESP works as well as searching for ways to help people control it.

One of the methods the center uses is known as the Ganzfeld technique. Feather says the goal of Ganzfeld experiments is to gain a better understanding of telepathy, and the technique is used primarily with two groups of people: those who have psychic experiences in their everyday lives and those who are highly creative. During a Ganzfeld test, a subject's task is to use mental telepathy to make the correct selection from four different images. First, the subject is coaxed into a relaxed state of consciousness by lying down in a comfortable reclining chair in a room that is illuminated by red light. To eliminate distracting sounds, earphones play white noise, which Feather describes as a "patternless, low-level background hiss."[66] Halved Ping-Pong balls are placed on

A Government ESP Secret

Throughout the years, government law enforcement agencies have publicly denounced the use of psychics. But for more than 20 years, the U.S. Defense Intelligence Agency spent over $20 million on a top-secret program called Stargate—and clairvoyance was at the heart of it. Stargate began in response to intelligence reports that the former Soviet Union was engaged in paranormal research. No one knew whether the research had yielded results, but U.S. officials saw clairvoyance (referred to as *remote viewing*) as a way of

the subject's eyes so the only light that can be seen is diffused and soft pink. This helps the subject relax and creates a uniform visual field that allows him or her to see mental pictures more easily. According to Feather, experiment participants say that after spending a few minutes in this environment, "the red glow and static noise appear to vanish from conscious awareness."[67]

During the first 10 minutes of a Ganzfeld session, the subject hears quiet relaxation suggestions through the earphones. Then mentally spying on the Soviets or anyone else who was considered a threat to the United States. An engineer named Hal Puthoff was selected to head the program, and working out of Fort Meade, Maryland, he recruited a team of remote viewers from the military to fill the role of "psychic spies." Over the life of the Stargate program, more than 250 projects were conducted, and some were highly successful. Remote viewers predicted an Iraqi attack on an American warship 48 hours in advance, helped locate a kidnapped U.S. Marine Corps officer in Europe, and aided in the search for biological and nuclear material and weapons in North Korea. Reviews about the project's success rate were mixed, however, and Stargate was ended in 1996.

a sender, who is located in a separate room (often in another part of the building), watches a short video clip and then mentally encourages the subject to visualize and describe it. The subject is encouraged to free-associate, or talk spontaneously about whatever images have formed in his or her mind. At the same time, an experimenter records whatever the subject says, and the sender listens through earphones. After the session has ended, the subject looks at four different video clips—the one the sender actually watched and three decoys—and then chooses the clip that most resembles his or her mental imagery.

Feather says that Ganzfeld experiments have been very successful at the research center. She says that subjects seem to do best at choosing correct video clips when the film shows dynamic scenes with motion and sound. Another finding is that ESP seems to work best when the subject and sender are either related to each other or are close friends. "These Ganzfeld tests for ESP are technical and complicated," she says, "but they are necessary if you want the scientific community or other careful, cautious individuals to consider the results as evidence of the paranormal. Tests like these allow us to continue to feel confident that ESP is a real phenomenon. We have the evidence."[68]

Telephone Telepathy

Rupert Sheldrake has also performed experiments to test for telepathy, and many of them involved the telephone. Sheldrake says that the most common kind of telepathy takes place in connection with telephone calls. As he explains: "About 80 percent of the population claim to have had experiences in which they think of someone for no apparent reason, then that person calls; or they know who is calling when the phone rings, before picking it up."[69] Over the past few years, Sheldrake has conducted hundreds of controlled experiments to investigate telephone telepathy, and he regularly videotapes the sessions. During a typical experiment, he asks each of his subjects to give him the names and telephone numbers of four people to whom they are close, such as family members or friends who would be most likely to call them. He tosses a set of dice to randomly select one of the chosen callers and then telephones the person, giving him or her instructions to wait five minutes and then call the subject. When the phone rings, the subject tries to guess which caller it is before lifting the receiver.

Sheldrake says that he has been amazed by the results of the telepathy experiments. By chance, the subjects should have made correct guesses one time out of four, which would be a success rate of 25 percent. The actual results, however, are much better; the subjects are correct about 45 percent of the time. According to Sheldrake, this is "massively significant statistically with odds against chance of . . . more than a billion to one."[70] He has expanded his telepathy studies to include email communication, and he is also conducting a worldwide experiment using the Internet.

Animal Studies

In addition to his experiments to test for ESP in humans, Sheldrake has also performed tests to better understand the sixth sense in animals. One of those experiments involved an African gray parrot named N'kisi (pronounced "in-key-see"). The parrot's owner, Aimee Morgana, claimed that N'kisi had the ability to respond to her thoughts and intentions telepathically. She had spent a great deal of time teaching the parrot to talk, and by the time he was 5 years old, he had a vocabulary of more than 700 words and was able to speak in complete sentences using correct grammar. But it was his ability to understand things before they happened that Morgana found most amazing, as she explains: "I was thinking of calling Rob, and picked up the phone to do so, and N'kisi said, 'Hi, Rob,' as I had the phone in my hand and was moving toward the Rolodex to look up his number." Morgana says that an even more remarkable incident happened one day while she was taking a nap on the couch. She was dreaming that

To see how lions interact and behave, you have to observe them in their natural habitat. To understand ESP, we have to look at how it manifests itself spontaneously outside the laboratory in daily life."

— Researcher
Sally Rhine Feather
discusses
studying ESP.

she was in the bathroom holding a brown medicine bottle, and N'kisi woke her up by saying, "See, that's a bottle."[71]

To test the parrot's telepathic abilities, Sheldrake set up experiments in Morgana's home in New York City, with video cameras taping the action. During one experiment, with the parrot in his cage, Morgana went to a separate room on a different floor and hooked up a nursery monitor so she could hear what N'kisi said. She was given a sealed envelope that had a pack of cards with pictures on them inside. She selected a card from the pack that showed a girl, and then she silently concentrated on the card. According to Sheldrake, N'kisi called out clearly and distinctly, "That's a girl."[72] After a total of 149 tests, the parrot had succeeded in guessing correctly 71 times, which led Sheldrake to conclude that N'kisi did indeed have the ability to communicate telepathically with his owner.

Mind Over Matter

Dean Radin has also spent many years testing for psychic powers, but his experiments have focused on humans. Radin, who is a senior scientist at the Institute for Noetic Sciences in Petaluma, California, is convinced that some psychic experiences are genuine, and that many people have actually had such experiences. He is a realist, however, and refers to people who claim to have extremely reliable or accurate psychic abilities as delusional. "This topic is exploited for entertainment purposes," he says, "and the world is full of unscrupulous individuals who falsely claim psychic abilities, so I understand why many scientists avoid this topic." Radin adds, though, that there is convincing evidence about ESP, and it has been proven that some psychic effects can be repeatedly observed during experiments under controlled conditions. He believes this is a sign that scientific assumptions about human capacities are seriously flawed. He explains: "There is certainly room for scholarly debate about these topics, and I know many informed skeptics whose opinions I value. However, I've also learned that there are some who are irrationally hostile about this topic, yet they know little or nothing about it."[73]

Radin has devoted much of his career to studying psychic phenomena. Many of his experiments have been designed to prove that the human mind has the power to influence objects, including computers and other machines. In one experiment, subjects used their minds to flip a "psychic switch," or mentally manipulate a clawlike robotic arm called "Robix." The robot's task was to pick up a red peanut M&M and drop it into a small cup. Based on about 1,000 of these experiments, Radin determined that when Robix was not being watched, he could complete the job in about 25 steps. When a human was involved in the task, however, the robot had completed the job in as few as two steps—a convincing sign that its actions were being influenced by the human mind.

Before Radin moved to California, he worked as a scientist in Las Vegas, Nevada, and journalist Chip Brown visited his research laboratory to participate in one of his experiments with the robot. Brown sat in front of a computer, and when Radin gave him the go-ahead, he hit the return key, which he says caused Robix to "wheeze and twitch." He had no idea what would happen or what to expect, as he explains:

> How [do you do it]? Well, any way you want, apparently, as long as you don't hit Robix, which,

as you quickly discover, is intensely tempting. Radin encourages participants to express emotions. I tried some hard frowning, as if Robix were a child. . . . Shazam! The obedient puppet plucked and delivered the M&M in 17 steps. . . . Maybe Robix was picking up my confusion, because in the second round it [was] just hovering over the M&M. I tried yelling "Come on!" but that was as effective as giving orders to a cat.[74]

As hard as he focused, Brown could not get Robix to obey his mental instructions again. He finally concentrated hard and caused the robot to move, but this time it took Robix 35 steps to get the M&M in the cup.

Radin himself participated in a different type of mind-over-matter experiment: using only his mind to bend a heavy silver-plated spoon. Of all the research he has done, and as convinced as he is about the existence of psychic phenomena, he was skeptical for many years about people who claimed they could bend spoons just by tapping into mental powers. But he was curious enough to attend a spoon-bending gathering in 2000—and to his amazement, he was able to accomplish the feat himself. As he concentrated on his spoon, he noticed that the spoon's bowl began to feel pliable, as though it were made of modeling clay or putty instead of metal. Then, with very little effort, he easily bent the bowl using only his thumb and one finger. Quickly the misshapen spoon hardened again and felt cold to the touch. Curious about whether he had unconsciously forced the bowl to bend, he immediately checked his fingers for noticeable marks, but none existed. He also examined the bend in the spoon to check for cracking or discoloration that would indicate the bend had been forced, but again, no such signs. It was obvious to Radin that he had bent the spoon using nothing more than his mind. "I have no easy explanation for this phenomenon," he says, "but I cannot deny my own experience. This bend was not due to a conjuring trick or to enhanced strength."[75]

Mind Experiments

Like Radin, Robert G. Jahn, a scientist with Princeton University, has spent years performing mind-over-matter experiments. But in the same way that J.B. Rhine shied away from terms such as *spiritualism* and *séance*, Jahn has purposely avoided words such as *paranormal*, *psychic*, and *parapsychology*. Instead, he refers to his science as *engineering anomalies*, which is why he chose the name Princeton Engineering Anomalies Research (PEAR) for his laboratory.

Since the 1970s Jahn and other scientists at PEAR have performed thousands of experiments involving random-event generator machines, which can be compared to electronic coin flippers. The machines, which are about the size of toaster ovens, are designed to come up with equal numbers of heads and tails. But when an operator sits in front of a machine, it is possible

James Randi insists that repeatable experiments are absolutely necessary to prove the existence of ESP. He is a well-known stage magician and a vocal skeptic of psychic phenomena.

for the results to be influenced by the person's mind. Volunteers have performed the experiments in the PEAR laboratory in New Jersey as well as in other locations, including other buildings, different cities or states, or even distant countries such as Hungary, Kenya, Brazil, and India. No matter how far away the participants were from the lab, they, too, were able to influence the machine's output using only their minds.

Although PEAR closed in February 2007, the scientists who worked there performed ESP experiments for nearly 30 years. According to Jahn, they made significant progress in that time, and he is confident that others will carry on the work they started. "It's time for a new era," he says, "for someone to figure out what the implications of our results are for human culture, for human study, and—if the findings are correct—what they say about our basic scientific attitude."[76]

"Is It Proof?"

From Ganzfeld tests to mind-over-matter experiments, from spoon bending to telepathy experiments in parrots, the powers of the mind are a source of fascination for the scientists who study extrasensory perception. Theirs is a field that has many avid supporters as well as skeptics who believe that what they do is a complete waste of time. Yet psychic phenomena continue to be pursued, studied, and analyzed by people who hope that one day they will unlock the mysteries of ESP so it will become as accepted as any other branch of science. Michael Schmicker shares this perspective:

> The paranormal phenomena . . . are obviously quirky, unpredictable, and poorly understood. But

the scientific evidence for their existence, as we have seen, is substantial and often impressive. Is it proof? That's your call. But it seems safe to say that the evidence is good enough to allow an intelligent, educated person to conclude, without embarrassment or apology, that at least some paranormal phenomena exist, and that their ultimate explanation may require rewriting science.[77]

NOTES

Introduction: The Sixth Sense

1. Quoted in Sally Rhine Feather and Michael Schmicker, *The Gift: ESP, the Extraordinary Experiences of Ordinary People.* New York: St. Martin's, 2005, p. 174.
2. Quoted in Alison George, "Take Nobody's Word for It," *New Scientist*, December 9, 2006, p. 56(2).

Chapter 1: The Roots of ESP

3. Michael Schmicker, *Best Evidence*. Lincoln, NE: Writers Club, 2002, p. 231.
4. Schmicker, *Best Evidence*, p. 231.
5. Jon Klimo, *Channeling: Investigations on Receiving Information from Paranormal Sources.* New York: St. Martin's, 1987, p. 95.
6. Quoted in Klimo, *Channeling*, p. 99.
7. Quoted in Schmicker, *Best Evidence*, p. 91.
8. Quoted in Schmicker, *Best Evidence*, p. 238.
9. Schmicker, *Best Evidence*, p. 239.
10. Feather and Schmicker, *The Gift*, p. 8.
11. Quoted in Feather and Schmicker, *The Gift*, p. 11.
12. Schmicker, *Best Evidence*, p. 66.

Chapter 2: Strange and Unexplained

13. Quoted in Caskets on Parade, "'The Wreck of the Titan,'... or 'Futility' by Morgan Robertson." www.msu.edu.
14. Quoted in John Gross, "Books of the Times: The Wreck of the Titanic Foretold?" *New York Times*, March 14, 1986. http://query.nytimes.com Senan Molony, "Just How Much of a Prophet Was Morgan Robertson?" Titanic Book Site, March 18, 2003. www.titanicbooksite.com.
16. Alexander Golbin, "A Tribute to the Most Mystic Figure of the 20th Century—the Unusual Mind and Unusual Talent of Wolf Messing," *Sleep & Health Newsletter*, May/June 2004. www.sleepandhealth.com.
17. Dana Landers, interview with author, December 11, 2006.
18. Landers, interview.
19. Becky Vollink, interview with author, February 7, 2007.
20. Vollink, interview.
21. Vollink, interview.
22. Vollink, interview.
23. Sylvia Browne and Antoinette May, *Adventures of a Psychic*. Carlsbad, CA: Hay House, 1990, p. 11.
24. Browne and May, *Adventures of a Psychic*, p. 12.
25. Browne and May, *Adventures of a Psychic*, p. 12.
26. Browne and May, *Adventures of a Psychic*, p. xi.

Chapter 3: Psychic Detectives

27. Quoted in Noreen Renier: Psychic Detective, "Testimonials." http://noreenrenier.com.

28. Quoted in Darrell Laurant, "Psychic Noreen Renier: 'It's Very Draining, What I Do,'" *Lynchburg News & Advance*, July 31, 2005. www.newsadvance.com.

29. Quoted in Emanuella Grinberg, "In Last Efforts to Find Laci, a Psychic, a Sweatshirt, and a Shoe," Court TV, July 22, 2004. www.courttv.com.

30. Quoted in Douane D. James, "A Psychic Sleuth," *Gainesville Sun*, May 1, 2003. http://noreenrenier.com.

31. Quoted in *On the Record with Greta Van Susteren*, "Interview with Psychic Investigator Noreen Renier," transcript, Fox News, April 29, 2003. http://noreenrenier.com.

32. Quoted in *CNN.com*, "Psychic Detectives," transcript, May 30, 2005. http://transcripts.cnn.com.

33. Quoted in James, "A Psychic Sleuth."

34. Joe Nickell, "Police 'Psychics': Do They Really Help Solve Crimes?" Committee for the Scientific Investigation of Claims of the Paranormal. www.csicop.org.

35. Benjamin Radford, "Despite Popularity, Psychic Detectives Fail to Perform," *Live Science*, February 4, 2005. www.livescience.com.

36. Quoted in Radford, "Despite Popularity, Psychic Detectives Fail to Perform."

37. Quoted in Geoff Gray, "Psychic Ops," *New York*, January 21, 2002. http://nymag.com.

38. Katherine Ramsland, "Early Cases," *All About Psychic Detectives*, Court TV Crime Library. www.crimelibrary.com.

39. Quoted in *CNN.com*, "Psychic Detectives," transcript, November 23, 2005. http://transcripts.cnn.com.

40. Quoted in *CNN.com*, "Psychic Detectives," November 23, 2005.

41. Quoted in *San Francisco Chronicle*, "Crime-Solving Duo Uses Psychic, Practical Skills," September 9, 2005. www.sfgate.com.

42. Quoted in Matt King, "'Medium' Knows the Message," *Gilroy Dispatch*, December 30, 2004. www.gilroydispatch.com.

43. Quoted in King, "'Medium' Knows the Message."

44. Quoted in Carole Braden, "Real-Life 'Mediums': Can Crimes Really Be Solved Using Psychic Powers?" *Good Housekeeping*, November 2005, pp. 123(3).

45. Quoted in CNN.com, "Psychic Detectives," May 30, 2005.

Chapter 4: Do Animals Have ESP?

46. Quoted in Rupert Sheldrake, "Listen to the Animals," *Ode Magazine*, July 2005. www.odemagazine.com.

47. Quoted in James M. Deem, "ESP Story 1: Animal Psychics?" James M. Deem Story Museum. www.jamesmdeem.com.

48. Rupert Sheldrake, *Dogs That Know When Their Owners Are Coming Home*. New York: Three Rivers, 1999, p. 2.

49. Quoted in Sheldrake, *Dogs That Know When Their Owners Are Coming Home*, p. 66.

50. Quoted in Sheldrake, *Dogs That Know When Their Owners Are Coming Home*, p. 68.

51. Quoted in Sheldrake, *Dogs That Know When Their Owners Are Coming Home*, p. 262.

52. Quoted in Sheldrake, *Dogs That Know When Their Owners Are Coming Home*, p. 261.

53. Quoted in Monica Collins, "Incredible Journey," Boston.com, January 30, 2005. www.boston.com.

54. Rupert Sheldrake, "The Unexplained Powers of Animals," *New Renaissance Magazine*, Spring 2003. www.ru.org.

55. John Roach, "Internal Clock Leads Monarch Butterflies to Mexico," *National Geographic News*, June 10, 2003. http://news.nationalgeographic.com.

56. Quoted in Burl Burlingame, "Man Talks to Animals—and They Talk Back," *Honolulu Star Bulletin*, February 26, 2000. www.rense.com.

57. Quoted in Burlingame, "Man Talks to Animals—and They Talk Back."

58. Quoted in Burlingame, "Man Talks to Animals—and They Talk Back."

59. Quoted in Burlingame, "Man Talks to Animals—and They Talk Back."

Chapter 5: Studying ESP

60. Parapsychological Association, "Frequently Asked Questions." www.parapsych.org.

61. James Randi Educational Foundation, "FAQs: One Million Dollar Paranormal Challenge," 2006. www.randi.org.

62. Schmicker, *Best Evidence*, p. 104.

63. Schmicker, *Best Evidence*, p. 106.

64. Feather and Schmicker, *The Gift*, p. xiii.

65. Feather and Schmicker, *The Gift*, pp. xi–xii.

66. Feather and Schmicker, *The Gift*, p. 14.

67. Sally Rhine Feather, "Recent Experimental Studies: Telepathy Study," The Rhine Research Center. www.rhine.org.

68. Feather and Schmicker, *The Gift*, p. 16.

69. Rupert Sheldrake, "Gosh, I Was Just Thinking About You," *Times* (London), September 7, 2006. www.sheldrake.org.

70. Quoted in Robyn Williams, "In Conversation: Rupert Sheldrake," ABC Radio National, October 5, 2006. www.abc.net.

71. Rupert Sheldrake and Aimee Morgana, "Testing a Language-Using Parrot for Telepathy," *Journal of Scientific Exploration*, 2003, pp. 601–15.

72. Quoted in Sheldrake and Morgana, "Testing a Language-Using Parrot for Telepathy," pp. 601–15.

73. Dean Radin, "Bio." www.deanradin.com.

74. Chip Brown, "They Laughed at Galileo Too," *New York Times*, August 11, 1996. www.chipbrown.net.

75. Dean Radin, "Consciousness Research Laboratory: Mind-Matter Interaction Phenomena," August 21, 2005. www.deanradin.com.

76. Quoted in Benedict Carey, "After 28 Years, Princeton Loses ESP Lab," *New York Times*, February 10, 2007, p. A1.

77. Schmicker, *Best Evidence*, p. 272.

GLOSSARY

automatic writing: The act of writing or typing material without the control of the conscious self.

channeling: Psychic communication with the spirit world.

clairvoyance: The power of seeing visions of people, actions, or events in clear detail, often at great distances (sometimes called remote viewing).

levitate: To be suspended in the air.

monotheism: The belief that there is only one deity or god.

Ouija board: A type of game board with letters and numbers that is used by people who are attempting to communicate with ghosts or spirits.

paranormal: Phenomena that defy the laws of natural science, such as ESP.

parapsychology: The scientific study of psychic powers.

precognition: The ability to see things in one's mind before they actually happen.

prophet: Someone, often a religious person, who can predict the future.

retrofitting: Applying after-the-fact matching of beliefs or observations to past events.

séance: The gathering of a group of people for the purpose of contacting spirits of the dead.

Spiritualism: A mid–nineteenth-century movement that focused on the afterlife and communication with the spirit world.

telepathy: The ability to send and receive messages using only the mind.

Zener cards: A special deck of cards used for testing for telepathic or clairvoyant skills.

FOR FURTHER RESEARCH

Books

Jessica Adams, *Psychic Powers: Do You Have a Secret Sixth Sense?* London: Hodder & Stoughton, 2004. Encourages readers to develop their sixth sense by getting in touch with their natural psychic powers as well as by learning how to make their powers stronger through tips and exercises.

Dawn Baumann Brunke, *Awakening to Animal Voices: A Teen Guide to Telepathic Communication with All Life.* Rochester, VT: Bindu, 2004. Using games, exercises, and experiments, this book teaches teens how to use telepathy to connect with animals and the world at large in a deeper, more meaningful way.

Maureen Caudill, *Suddenly Psychic: A Skeptic's Journey.* Charlottesville, VA: Hampton Roads, 2006. The author, who is a scientist, writes about the years she spent being skeptical about ESP and how her views radically changed once she began having her own experiences with channeling, remote viewing, and other psychic phenomena.

Bill Hewitt, *Psychic Development for Beginners: An Easy Guide for Releasing and Developing Your Psychic Abilities.* St. Paul, MN: Llewellyn, 2002. This book features more than 25 examples and numerous mental exercises designed to help people develop their natural powers of psychic healing, telepathy, clairvoyance, channeling, and psychometry, among others.

Rupert Sheldrake, *Dogs That Know When Their Owners Are Coming Home.* New York: Three Rivers, 1999. Using real-life examples, the author, who is a scientist, presents his theories about dogs and other animals that have senses that cannot be explained by conventional science.

Periodicals

Keith Harary, "Mind Games," *Psychology Today*, November/December 2005. A man who has been called "superpsychic" discusses parapsychology and inexplicable powers.

Sarah Mahoney, "Going with Your Gut," *Prevention*, July 2006. An article that explains how it is possible to make one's sixth sense just as strong as the five natural senses.

Internet Sources

James Carpenter, "Why Parapsychology Now?" *Journal of Parapsychology*, December 2002. www.rhine.org/texts/bed1126.htm. Written by a parapsychologist who shares many anecdotes about people's real-life experiences with ESP.

Joe Nickell, "Investigative Files: Psychic Pets and Pet Psychics," *Skeptical Inquirer*, November/December 2002. www.csicop.org/si/2002-11/pet-psychic.html. An article by one of the most outspoken ESP skeptics, who writes that none of the claims about animals having psychic powers has ever been proven and is not supported by scientific investigation.

Kevin Poulsen, "Skeptic Revamps $1M Psychic Prize," *Wired News*, January 12, 2007. www.wired.com/news/technology/1,72482-0.html. This article discusses the large cash prize offered by ESP skeptic James Randi to anyone who can prove that he or she possesses psychic, paranormal, or supernatural abilities.

Katherine Ramsland, "All About Psychic Detectives," Court TV Crime Library. www.crimelibrary.com/criminal_mind/forensics/psychics/index.html. A well-written, interesting minibook about criminal investigations and how law enforcement agencies have used people with psychic powers to help them solve cases.

Web Sites

About.com: Paranormal Phenomena (http://paranormal.about.com). This information-packed site includes "true stories" of ESP experiences, numerous articles related to the paranormal, and links to everything from life after death to witchcraft and spells.

How Stuff Works (http://science.howstuffworks.com). Young people who are interested in ESP will find various articles on this site, including "How ESP Works," "How Hypnosis Works," and "How Nostradamus Works," among others.

James Randi Educational Foundation (www.randi.org). The official site of stage magician and staunch ESP skeptic James Randi, whose educational foundation aims to "promote critical thinking by reaching out to the public and media with reliable information about paranormal and supernatural ideas so widespread in our society today."

Rhine Research Center (www.rhine.org). This site includes a wealth of information related to parapsychology, including a glossary of terms, reading suggestions, links to articles, recent ESP studies, and a message board.

Index

animal studies of, 79–80

telepathy experiments of, 78–79

Shizuru, Wayne, 68–69

Smart, Elizabeth, 49–50

Smith, Etta, 54

Society for Psychical Research (SPR), 21–23

Southeast Asian tsunami (2004), 56–57

Spiritualism, 13–16

Stalin, Joseph, 33, 34

telepathy, 25

animals endowed with, 59–60

experiments in, 75–78

Titanic, 30

Uribe, Melanie, 54

Vinger, Tom, 50

Vollink, Becky, 37–39

Walsh, Jay, 63–64

Walsh, Nicole, 63–64

Wegener, Alfred, 9

The Wreck of the Titanic Foretold? (Gardner), 30

Zener cards, 24, 26

About the Author

Peggy J. Parks holds a bachelor of science degree from Aquinas College in Grand Rapids, Michigan, where she graduated magna cum laude. She is a freelance author who has written more than 50 nonfiction books for children and young adults. Parks lives in Muskegon, Michigan, a town that she says inspires her writing because of its location on the shores of Lake Michigan.